# Blair Witch
## Book of Shadows

# Blair Witch
## Book of Shadows

D.A. Stern

POCKET BOOKS
New York  London  Toronto  Sydney  Singapore

The following is based on actual events. Some
dramatic re-creation was necessary for reasons
that will become obvious.

Photos and illustrations except on the following
pages Courtesy of Artisan Entertainment.

An *Original* Publication of Pocket Books

POCKET BOOKS, a division of Simon & Schuster, Inc.
1230 Avenue of the Americas, New York, NY 10020

ISBN: 0-7434-1189-7

First Pocket Books trade paperback printing November 2000

10 9 8 7 6 5 4 3 2 1

POCKET and colophon are registered trademarks of Simon & Schuster, Inc.

Printed in the U.S.A

# Introduction

Pop quiz.

What's the single most frightening image from your childhood?

Take your time and think back to the stories you read, or those that were read to you, the cartoons and films you saw on television or in the theater, even those first few Halloweens you spent holding tight to your mother's or father's hand as wave after wave of frighteningly costumed big kids walked by.

Got it yet?

Okay. Pencils down.

I'll lay odds that a significant portion of you picked the Wicked Witch of the West, from *The Wizard of Oz*.

Of course, it wasn't just the image—the green skin, pointed hat, crooked nose—that made the witch so terrifying. What really sealed the deal was her laugh.

In a book called *The Making of The Wizard of Oz* (Knopf, 1977) actress Margaret Hamilton, who portrayed the witch, remembered that virtually everyone she met wanted her to do the laugh.

"Sometimes when I go to schools," Hamilton told author Aljean Harmetz, "if we're in an auditorium, I'll do it. And there's always a funny reaction, like *Ye Gods, they wish they hadn't asked*. They're scared. They're really scared."

That's an image worth considering a moment: a few hundred adolescents crowded into a brightly lit school auditorium, looking around nervously, suddenly face-to-face with their most frightening childhood memory. An audience united by a common thread of belief, primed to explode in hysterics should someone choose that moment to, say, switch out the auditorium lights?

All right. Now set aside that image for this one:

A nine-year-old boy, sitting alone in the forest, as night descends, with only his childhood nightmares for company. The central image in his dreams is a figure out of legend to rival the crooked-nose Wicked Witch of the West, one that he believes haunts these very woods.

That figure, we won't name just yet.

But we can call the boy Jeff Patterson.

The name that may ring a bell with some of you, thanks to the recent series of events the press has dubbed "The Black Hills Murders." Jeff and his accomplices in those murders, some say, were themselves primed to explode, inspired by their common belief in the supernatural force that lives in the Black Hills.

Some of you may be similarly primed to believe the stories now being issued by Patterson, Kim Diamond, Stephen Ryan Parker, and their representatives, that the force in that woods really does exist, and is responsible for the killings the three stand accused of.

One thing is for certain: in the coming months, there are those who will debate the issue ad nauseum, sifting through every piece of evidence related to the case—the diaries, the phone calls, the e-mails, the interviews— to find hidden nuances, secret meaning, in the hope that the discussion itself will point them in new directions, or reveal the truth behind the mystery.

To which we say, sometimes discussion, analysis, and debate does serve a purpose.

And sometimes, it's better to let the evidence speak for itself.

—D.A. Stern

Las Vegas, Nevada

October 4, 1999 $3.50

# U.S.A. REPORT

Accused killers Kim Diamond
and Stephen Parker

## Thrill Kills

A bloody crime spree in the
Black Hills leaves eight dead and
a nation wondering what evil
lurks in the heart of the forest

**Broadway Is Back!**
Singing Sensation Kara
Grenier Lights Up the Great White Way

# MASSACRE IN M

## Did a local legend inspire a series of Manson-esque killings?

By Clement Duritz

It would be a horrifying enough tale taken out of context, a *Gilligan's Island* gone bad for the new millennium. Five young people on an overnight camping trip, hopped up on a mixture of drugs and alcohol, take six innocent lives. Then the group turns upon itself, resulting in two more deaths. A bloody, shocking series of events.

But what takes the killings beyond the horrifying into the macabre is their locale: the Black Hills of Maryland, an isolated patch of wooded wilderness an hour west of Washington D.C. made famous in the hit movie *The Blair Witch Project*. That motion picture documented the disappearance of student filmmakers Heather Donahue, Joshua Leonard, and Michael Williams in those woods, all supposed victims of local bogeyman—or in this case, bogeywoman—the Blair Witch.

Those inclined to a belief in the supernatural can now add the names Jeffrey Patterson, Kim Diamond, Stephen Ryan Parker, Erica Geerson, and Tristen Ryler to the Blair Witch mythology. All five were participants in what the local media has dubbed "The Black Hills Murders," which took place the week of September 20. That Friday night, Patterson, himself a resident of Burkittsville, Maryland, the witch's supposed hometown, led the others into those very same hills on his inaugural "Blair Witch Hunt"—a guided tour of those sites commonly associated with the local legend. According to some, Patterson's "hunt" was all too successful; it is the Blair Witch, these people believe, who is behind the latest round of killings.

The authorities seem to prefer other, more mundane explanations. They have arrested Patterson, Diamond, and Parker on first-degree murder charges. All three now sit in Rockville State Prison, awaiting trial. The cases against them are airtight, sources say, supported by physical evidence that includes actual videotapes of at least two of the killings. At press time, all the

major network television newsmagazines were rumored to be bidding for the right to air those tapes.

Jeff Patterson spent the afternoon of September 20 giving his charges a thorough tour of the sites historically associated with the Blair Witch (*see sidebar*). As part of that tour, the group donned backpacks and set out into the Black Hills State Forest. Their destination: the ruined foundation of Rustin Parr's house. Locals

involved in the burgeoning Blair Witch tourist industry point to this spot as the plum attraction on any sightseeing trip. Patterson and his group arrived there close to sunset, and set up camp.

According to Burkittsville Sheriff Ronald Cravens, sometime in the early evening Patterson's tour group was confronted by another, run by locals Tony Amonte and Nicholas Dugan. Amonte and Dugan laid claim to camping rights in the foundation, and angry words were exchanged. Eventually the newcomers, accompanied by tourists Greta Hanson, John Chin, and E.J. Kim, stalked off. The Parr site secured, Patterson and company settled in and began consuming considerable amounts of alcohol and hal-

lucinogens. Fuel for what came next, according to Cravens.

The sheriff believes that sometime in the predawn hours, Parker, Patterson, and at least one other member of the group trekked through the woods to Coffin Rock, where Amonte and Dugan's group were sleeping. There, they murdered all five hikers in their sleep, arranging their disemboweled bodies in the shape of a pentagram to simulate the "Coffin Rock Massacre" of 1886.

Stephen Ryan Parker would have known the exact details of those century-old killings better than most. Parker, an award-winning folklore expert, had come to the Black Hills with coauthor and live-in girlfriend Tristen Ryler to research *The Blair Witch: Hysteria or History?* A serious, scholarly man who saved his passion for his work, Parker, according to friends, was under

tremendous stress in the weeks leading up to his Black Hills trip. One reason was his looming book deadline: another, the state of his relationship with Ryler. The two had been having bitter fights with increasing frequency. Parker hoped, according to friends, to use the trip as a chance to patch things up between them. What the couple's friends didn't know was that Tristen Ryler, who left her Cambridge, Massachusetts, home on the morning of September 20, was six weeks pregnant.

Authorities remain shocked by Parker's involvement in the Black Hills killings, citing his character and previously spotless record. They evince no such surprise in the case of Chicago native Kim Diamond. At the ripe old age of 21, Diamond, a member of the same Goth culture taken to task by the media for its supposed role in the Columbine shootings, already had a  long history of trouble with the law. In addition to misdemeanor drug possession charges, her record included two extended stints at Camp LaGauge, a juvenile detention facility run like a boot camp, just outside Waukegan. Even there, Diamond was a disruptive influence, according to a camp official: "A time bomb, just waiting to explode."

The morning of Thursday, September 21, Tristen Ryler awoke to discover that; during the night, possibly because of stress suffered during the previous night's events, she had suffered a miscarriage. She was rushed to a nearby hospital, treated and released. The entire Blair Witch Hunt tour group then returned to Jeff Patterson's home which is located near the Black Hills.

What they did during the day is not yet known, but Kim Diamond's movements during the early evening hours are easy to trace. Several witnesses—as well as videotapes from a security camera—place her in the Black Hills Market, a local convenience store, where she

# CURSE OF THE BLAIR WITCH?

**1639** Colonel Nathan Blair founds the township of Blair, Maryland. A week later, he dies in bed.

**February 1785** Elly Kedward, the supposed "Blair Witch," is condemned to death by the townspeople of Blair.

**November 1786** The children of Blair disappear en masse. Residents, fearing a curse, abandon the town.

**January 1809** *The Blair Witch Cult,* an eyewitness account of the Kedward affair, is published.

**August 1823** The town of Burkittsville is founded on the ruins of old Blair.

**August 1825** Eileen Treacle, 11, drowns in Tappy

East Creek. Witnesses testify an old woman pulled her under.

**March 1886** Five men, sent out to recover a missing 8-year-old girl, are found disemboweled at Coffin Rock, tied together at the arms and legs in the shape of a pentagram.

**May 1941** Rustin Parr, a mildly retarded local hermit, confesses to the brutal murder of seven children—

# Hysteria or History?

Investigative journalists are a funny breed: the very nature of their job sometimes requires them to become part of the story they are supposed to be impartially covering.

Pocket Books, an imprint of publishing titan Simon & Schuster, signed up Stephen Ryan Parker and Tristen Ryler to write a book on a recurring series of supposedly "supernatural" events that took place in Frederick County, Maryland, and the hysteria that accompanied them. But in no way could they have foreseen just how involved their authors would become in the Blair Witch mythos.

"We're all in a state of shock over the events of this past weekend," said Pocket Books President and Publisher Judith Curr. "It would be inappropriate for us to comment further at this point."

The book, *The Blair Witch: Hysteria or History?*, had been scheduled for publication in Summer 2001. But according to Jennifer Gates of the Zachary Shuster Agency, who repped Parker and Ryler's project to Pocket Books, the book was a huge hit at the company's recent sales conference, and Pocket approached the authors about finishing the book before their contractual due date of October 31, 2000, so that it could be rushed into stores sooner.

How close the book was to being finished remains a mystery, one not likely to be solved anytime soon. Yet industry insiders say that regardless of Parker and Ryler's progress on the manuscript, there is no doubt *The Blair Witch: Hysteria or History?* will be published before too long.

"They'll hire someone to do a quick rewrite and have the book on the shelves by Christmas, if not sooner—I guarantee it," said John Mutter of *Publishers Weekly*, considered the industry bible. "It's simply too hot a property for Pocket not to get it out there."

apparently went to replenish the group's alcohol supply. Diamond—dressed in full "goth" regalia, white face paint, head-to-toe black clothing—exchanged words with the store manager, Peggy Shuler, who refused to sell her groceries. Diamond then pulled out a nail file and slashed Shuler's throat, killing her.

Meanwhile, back at Patterson's home, relations among the other group members were souring. According to reports, Erica Geerson, 19, whose role in the weekend's events remains the most difficult to piece together, had been the object of sexual advances from Jeff Patterson throughout the course of the tour. She had repeatedly spurned him. At some point during the evening of September 21, authorities allege that a frustrated Patterson killed her in a jealous rage.

Rage is also the suspected motive behind the last of the Black Hills killings, Stephen Ryan Parker's murder of his coauthor and lover, Tristen Ryler. This murder was committed within Patterson's home on the evening of September 22, when, according to sources, Turner, in what he may have intended as a gruesome reenactment of the 1941 execution of Rustin Parr, hung Ryler from a makeshift gallows.

Though they hardly seem necessary, more details about the killings will no doubt flood newspapers, magazines, and television screens in the coming weeks. Some of those details will come from the mouths of the accused killers themselves, who have to this point refused all requests to talk with the media. Already there are signs that particular wall is cracking. Diamond is said to be making very loud, insistent claims from her jail cell that she is completely innocent, that she, Patterson, and Parker should in fact be looked upon as victims, set up to take the fall for the killings. Who committed these murders? Who else? The Blair Witch.

And what do the authorities think about Diamond's claim?

"You'll pardon my language, but that's a bunch of crap," Sheriff Cravens said when questioned. "There is no goddamn Blair Witch."

*Additional reporting by John Robinsky in Baltimore/Stefan Krc in New York*

the "Burkittsville Seven."

**Summer 1969** The Black Hills play host to a series of drug-induced rituals performed by a group of area hippies known as the "Blair Witch Cult," led by former rock 'n' roll musician Leroy Creegan.

**November 1983** Cece Malvey, a student at Johns Hopkins University, hangs himself after self-publishing a crude booklet called "Wood Witch Said," detailing stories supposedly told to him by the Blair Witch.

**MISSING**

On October 21, 1994, Heather Donahue, Joshua Leonard, and Michael Williams hiked into Maryland's Black Hills Forest to shoot a documentary film about the legendary "Blair Witch." They were never heard from again.

In the year since, their footage and their cars have been recovered, documenting the students' five-day journey through the Black Hills and capturing the terrifying events that led up to their disappearance.

**EVIDENCE EXISTS...**

• Audio and video footage of the students' terrifying journey through the Black Hills
• Interviews and testimonies of key witnesses
• The eventual hunt for missing filmmaker/director Heather Donahue

LOG ON TO www.blairwitch.com TO SEE AND HEAR

**October 1994** Heather Donahue, Joshua Leonard, and Michael Williams, three student filmmakers, disappear in the woods while filming a documentary on the Blair Witch.

**September 1999** The Black Hills murders.

# HYSTERIA OR HISTORY?

# POCKET BOOKS

**Simon & Schuster Consumer Group**
1230 Avenue of the Americas
New York, NY 10020

**Margaret A. Clark**
Executive Editor

January 12, 2000

D.A. Stern
P.O. Box 6566
Las Vegas, NV 89005

Dear Dave,

It was good to see you. It sounds like a lot of good things are happening.

Let me remind you about what we discussed. We had contracted last September with Stephen Ryan Parker and Tristen Ryler to write a book called *The Blair Witch: Hysteria or History?* For obvious reasons, they're not going to be able to finish that project.

We still think it's a viable idea, and we're looking for someone to take it over. Kara and Scott agree that you are the only author who could do the book justice. While Stephen and Tristen were pretty far along on the book, I'm not sure just how much of their material I'll be able to get hold of. You may be starting from scratch, but in light of recent events (and if I see just one more story on cable I'll scream) this could work to your advantage.

I'll look forward to hearing from you soon. As always, any questions, call or e-mail me.

Sincerely,

Margaret Clark
Executive Editor

## Clark, Margaret

**From:** dastern@mac.com
**Sent:** Tuesday, January 18, 2000 17:11:16 AM
**To:** Clark, Margaret
**Subject:** Blair Witch: Hysteria or History

Thanks for the kind words: I'm sure there are other people who could take on the project, but I'm happy to have the work. I had heard about Stephen and Tristen's book even before we talked (I'm fairly good friends with the woman who is their agent) and it sounded like a very interesting idea. Please do send on the material: use the Las Vegas P.O. Box.

I'll have Lisa call you to discuss the particulars <g>.

Dave

# THE BL[A...]

## HYST[...]

### HI[...]

B[...]

Stephen Rya[...]

Representation:

Jennifer Gates
Zachary Shuster Agency
888 Seventh Avenue
45th Floor
New York NY 10106

Margaret A. Clark

ZACHARY SHUSTER

A LITERARY & ENTERTAINMENT AGENCY

JENNIFER GATES

888 SEVENTH AVENUE, 45TH FLOOR, NEW YORK, NEW YORK 10106

Dave

Here's a printout and other related papers from my Hysteria or History file. Where's the rest of it? I'm trying to find out.

# THE BLAIR WITCH:

## HYSTERIA OR HISTORY?

## OVERVIEW

Hype? Or horror?

Fact? Or fairy tale?

Is there a real Blair Witch? Are the Black Hills of Western Maryland truly haunted? Or is the centuries-old supernatural presence people have claimed to encountered in those woods simply the latest, most frenzied example of the ages-old psychological phenomenon known as mass hysteria?

Since the spectacular success of the independent film *The Blair Witch Project* (made for somewhere between $10,000 and $100,000, depending on which reports you listen to, worldwide gross to date over $250 million), fans have flocked by the hundreds to the forest around Burkittsville, Maryland, searching for answers to those questions...and perhaps, a glimpse of the Witch herself.

Those same fans have clogged Internet chat rooms, and spent endless hours in debate over the most arcane aspects of the Blair Witch mythos. At this point, it is safe to say, literally millions of people across the globe are familiar with the names Rustin Parr, Elly Kedward, and Leroy Creegan...and want to know more about them.

The time is right, then, for a book that peels away the layers of myth that have built up around the Curse of the Blair Witch, a book that rigorously re-examines every part of the legend to arrive at the truth.

*The Blair Witch: Hysteria or History?* is that book. Using exclusive, never-before-published source documents, we will discuss each supposedly "supernatural" occurrence blamed on the Blair Witch, putting it in its proper historical and sociological context. We will present the hard evidence documenting the witch's existence—as well as the hallucinations and so-called "historical records" that have masqueraded as proof for centuries.

Our book will also place the legend of the Blair Witch itself in perspective, using actual trial records from the Great European Witch Hunts of the Middle Ages to demonstrate the archetypal nature of the hysteria surrounding the Blair Witch. Of particular note here is the story of "Bloody" Sam Caine, a supernatural figure said to have terrorized the Lancashire countryside in the 17th and 18th centuries.

We will also examine the role mob psychology played in the Inquisition and the Witch Hunts. Interviews and discussions with experts in the occult and group psychology will supplement our analysis, as will historical documents taken from a number of private collections that have agreed to grant us reproduction rights to their material.

## MANUSCRIPT LENGTH

90,000 words: completion date will be nine months from contract signing. Publication budget should provide for a sixteen-page black-and-white photo insert, as well as the services of a photo researcher.

## MARKET

The millions of fans who loved the film and bombarded the official Blair Witch website (www.blairwitch.com) with additional requests for information on the legend provide the core audience for this book. In addition, those turned off by the "homemade" look of the film but fascinated by the legend itself will no doubt flock to our book, as the success of other books that look behind the scenes of pop culture phenomenons (*The Physics of Star Trek, The Science of the X-Files,* etc.) demonstrates.

## COMPETITION

Most other books on the market today deal only with the film and its success, and the actual legend only incidentally (most notably, the original film tie-in *The Blair Witch Project Dossier*). This will be the first volume devoted specifically to the legend.

## ABOUT THE AUTHORS

Stephen Ryan Parker is a graduate of Yale University. The publication of his first book, *Beyond the Pale: The Extraordinary Life of Daniel Douglas Home,* coincided with his receipt of the prestigious Lomax Fellowship. Born and raised in Boston, he is hard at work on a collection of short essays, to be published by Harvard University Press in January of 2001.

Tristen Ryler is a graduate of Yale University, who now lives in Cambridge, Massachusetts. THE BLAIR WITCH: HYSTERIA OR HISTORY is her first published work.

# P O C K E T   B O O K S

**Simon & Schuster Consumer Group**
1230 Avenue of the Americas
New York, NY 10020

Margaret A. Clark
Executive Editor

August 25, 1999

Tristen Ryler
Stephen Ryan Parker
313 Kendall Common
Building 85
Cambridge MA 02141

Dear Stephen and Tristen:

Congratulations! I am delighted that we will be publishing *The Blair Witch: Hysteria or History?* here at Pocket. We're all looking forward to making the book as big a success in its own way as *The Blair Witch Project* was.

Your contract is making its way through our legal department right now (I'm sure Jennifer warned you about how long these things sometimes take), but in the meantime, I've enclosed some questionnaires our publicity department would like you to fill out. Please return them to my attention when you're finished.

Jennifer may also have shared with you my concerns about keeping this book accessible to a mainstream audience. I'm sure we'll talk more about this during the coming months, but I just want to mention here that I don't think a lot of people here in America will be buying *Hysteria or History* looking to read about Bloody Sam Caine, however colorful a figure he may have been.

I look forward to talking with you about the above at your earliest convenience.

Sincerely,

Margaret Clark
Executive Editor

From the desk of
**STEPHEN RYAN PARKER**

Ms. Clark:

Both Tristen and I understand your concerns about the academic nature of the project: we definitely want to avoid boring our audience. At the same time, I do feel it is important to establish that the Blair Witch legend did not arise out of a historical vacuum.

To wit: Bloody Sam Caine. Born Samuel Catlett Caine, from 1629 to 1634 a well-respected member of his Majesty's Court, having had the title "Witchfinder-General" bestowed upon him by Parliament. In April of 1635, however, Caine snaps, butchering five of his own assistants at Lancaster Castle.

He arranges their dead bodies in the shape of a pentagram.

I think you can see why the audience captivated by the Blair Witch might find Caine's story interesting as well. See the attached for details.

Give me a call if you want to discuss this issue further: you can also contact me via e-mail at lomaxfellow@coolmail.com

Best,

Stephen

are said to rendezvous at this point, as German witches are said to congregate for Sabbat in the Harz Mountains. GC. xii 187.

---

## BLOODY SAM CAINE

England's First Witchfinder-General, Samuel Catlett Caine.

Responsible for the prosecution and execution of close to a hundred "witches" during the early 1600s. Also blamed for a series of brutal killings at Lancaster Castle in 1635. Said to have bathed in the blood of his victims, and thus been granted immortality.

"A figure of such frightening aspect that Scratch himself trembled at the sight, and so snatched Caine's leg off when the man was sleeping that he might hear the clip-clop of his approach." Mainz and Heffen, *The Magical History of Lancashire County.*

In common usage, a figure of superstition, the boogeyman.

"Wouldst pluck out my innards, then, as if thee were Bloody Sam?"

DuBent's *Shropshire Witches,* Act III, Scene VI.

Black of Heart
Fore'er Damned
Beware the steel
Of Bloody Sam

Lancashire Folk-Rhyme, 1721. Notting and Whitley.
"Cold of heart," GC. iv 88
"By witch's curse," AP. i 32

---

## BOOK OF SHADOWS

A witch's spellbook. The phrase is believed to have originated with Merlin's legendary grimoire. GC. iii 65, AV. xxi 4

In Arthurian lore, the Book of Shadows was stolen by the Lady of the Lake when she imprisoned Merlin in a cave of glass. GC. iii 23

In Welsh sources, cf. the Black Book of Carmathen, *Llyfr o Cysgodion* is carried off by Merlin's Owl, Ambrosius, upon his master's imprisonment. LB. iii 25

# MODERN LIVING

## YOUTH

### TRUE BELIEVERS

Flip through the foot-high pile of articles on the Beatles' mid-decade conquest of America, and you'll find the word "hysteria" appears at least once in every single one of them. From New York to Washington, from Chicago to San Francisco, that hysteria seemed to spread like a virus: a young girl carted off on a stretcher here, another fainting in her concert seat there, elsewhere the band's limousine surrounded and frozen in place by screaming, seemingly senseless fans. New images of the insanity appeared virtually every day, flashing across television screens or splashed across the front pages of newspapers and magazines. Parents across America were stunned (perhaps forgetting their own bobby-soxed days of swooning over Frank Sinatra), authorities were scandalized, and the fans—usually young teenage girls—were often at a loss to explain the reasons for their behavior.

As the years passed, and the Beatles retreated from the concert stage to the recording studio, the hysteria—to the relief of all, including the band—seemed to fade. And now that the group has seemingly broken up, all traces of it (one would think) would finally be dispelled.

Not so fast.

In recent months, hysteria—albeit of an entirely different kind—has once again surrounded one of the group's members. Hysteria in the form of a rumor has spread like wildfire across the globe, a bizarre fiction taking on the appearance of reality, supported by the most insubstantial evidence imaginable. You may have heard it in passing on your radio, or seen a mention of it in the gossip columns, but in recent weeks the talk has reached a crescendo, till it now seems to be the number one topic of conversation among the youth of America.

"Everyone knows it," one young girl was overheard saying in a club recently. "Paul is dead."

Paul is Paul McCartney, of course, bass player and singer/songwriter extraordinaire, the voice of such hits as "Yesterday," "Can't Buy Me Love," and "Hey Jude." Or perhaps, not the latter, since Paul has been dead since 1966, killed in a London car crash. Want proof?

He's out of step, barefoot, and holding a cigarette in the wrong hand on the front cover of the *Abbey Road* record. He's facing the wrong way on the back of the *Sergeant Pepper* album. And if you listen closely to the end of the Beatles song "Strawberry Fields Forever," you can hear John Lennon saying "I buried Paul."

Where did this rumor come from? Blame Fred LaBour, a University of Michigan undergraduate, say some. It was his review of *Abbey Road* that first listed the telltale clues to Paul's untimely demise. Others point to a trio of disc jockeys from Detroit's WKNR-FM as the culprits. And there are other supposed sources as well, though it doesn't really matter who started the hysteria at this point; little, it seems, can be done to stop it. Particularly given recent events at New York's WABC, when disc jockey Roby Young was pulled off the air in the middle of enumerating those same clues mentioned above.

Proof of a vast conspiracy to some; another round of hysteria to others.

Count us here and now among the latter group: to those claiming Paul is dead, we say "bunk."

### FOLLOW THE LEADER

The Beatles, of course, were famous for "turning on" American youth to Eastern spiritualism, in the person of the Maharishi Mahesh Yogi. While the kings of pop were undertaking their famous 1967 spiritual pilgrimage to the Maharishi's Indian retreat, a Buffalo, New York, band called Hillary's Butterfly was honing its song-and-stagecraft on the more traditional rock 'n' roll touring circuit. The Butterfly finally broke through last year at about this time, when their single "Don't Start Nothin'" hit the national charts.

But shortly after achieving success, the group disbanded. Lead vocalist Leroy Creegan put down his microphone and picked up the spiritual mantle the Beatles had discarded. Last fall, Creegan, 27, moved to Jericho Mills, Maryland, and, accompanied by a core group of followers, set up a commune, one devoted to the enjoyment of nature and each other, judging by the principles laid out in their manifesto (some samples of their philosophy: "The earth is our mother," and "Sex is our reason for being"). And despite the predictable outbreaks of culture clash between twentieth-century hippies and nineteenth-century farmers (not to mention the ever-present—and never proven—accusations of drug abuse) Creegan's group, by all indications, have been good neighbors. That is, up until recently.

The problems began in late April, upon the arrival of warmer weather, when Creegan's group began performing a number of their rituals outdoors. That's when locals first realized that those ceremonies included elements drawn from the rich native folklore: Indian legends such as the Nanticoke Demon, believed by the area's original residents to haunt the surrounding forests, and the Blair Witch, a centuries-old ghost said to inhabit those same hills.

It's the association with the Blair Witch that has upset the previously harmonious relationship between Creegan and area residents. Many of them remember all too clearly the terrible winter of 1940-41, when seven children were kidnapped and brutally murdered by a local man who claimed to have been acting at the behest of the Blair Witch. Needless to say, they do not welcome any reminder of those times.

The fact these ceremonies virtually mimic those performed by a witches coven (the group, according to witnesses, congregates, disrobes, and reads from their so-called "prayer book") only adds fuel to the fire. Over the past month, police have had to respond on several different occasions to reports of trouble between locals and Creegan's group (who some in the press have taken to calling the "Blair Witch Cult"—another cause of friction between the two). In the interests of preserving peace, we suggest Creegan and his followers take a lesson from their own manifesto:

Words have power: do not use them hurtfully, or lightly.

CULT FIGURES    McCARTNEY

CREEGAN

**Maryland Historical Society**    140 N. Holliday Street    Baltimore MD 21307

Ms. Jane E. Coulter
Archive Director

September 6, 1999

Stephen Ryan Parker
313 Kendall Common
Building 85
Cambridge MA 02141

Dear Stephen:

I am writing with some distressing news.

During this past weekend's severe rainstorms, a portion of the ceiling in our main exhibit hall collapsed. Several of the items we had on display in the hall were damaged, including our copy of The Blair Witch Cult.

We have sent the book out to be restored, but because of its extreme age, the work is expected to take at least two months, during which time it will be unavailable for your use. I apologize for this inconvenience: I know we had promised you access to the book for your research, as well as the chance to reproduce portions of the Blair Witch Cult within your own book.

I will plan on contacting you again toward the beginning of November with an update on this situation. Or, if you prefer, I can put you directly in touch with the restoration house to discuss their progress.

Best,

Jane E. Coulter
Archive Director
Maryland Historical Society

jmg/JC

**Mother Demdike - The Infamous Lancashire Witch**
Woodcut courtesy The Salem Historical Foundation

Margaret:                    Sept 16

Sorry I sounded so out of it last time you called: I am not a morning person at all, and on top of that, I've been feeling pretty shitty these last few weeks. The flu, or something... I don't know. Anyway, Stephen and I are off to Minnesota this weekend and then, later this month, Burkittsville, where we'll be going on the "Blair Witch Hunt." Sounds cheesey to me, but Stephen talked to the guy running it and says it seems okay (here's the info). We'll see about that.

                    Tristen

Margaret Clark
Pocket Books
1230 6th Ave. 13th floor
NY, NY 10020

# Want to see Something Really Scary?

## The Blair Witch Hunt
Design: B. Buck Associates Frederick, Maryland

Stephen Ryan Parker
313 Kendall Common, Building 85
Cambridge MA 02141

c/o Margaret Clark
Pocket Books
1230 Avenue of the Americas
New York, NY 10020

Dear Ms Clark,

I know Stephen is still on the road doing research so as he suggested the last time we talked, I am sending this info to you.

I have finally managed to track down a copy of the November 1939 issue of TALES OF THE UNCANNY. As you may already be aware, this title has long had the reputation among collectors as being the hardest to find of the "weird menace" pulps. Its rarity stems from the fact that it was printed by Black Raven Press, a small Baltimore publisher that was in business for only a few years. Their magazines had poor distribution (most likely only in the mid-Atlantic states) and print runs were probably in the range of only 5,000 - 10,000 copies per issue.

UNCANNY is especially prized by collectors today because their lineup of contributors included such luminaries as H. P. Lovecraft, Clark Ashton Smith and many other noteworthy authors. Although the magazine didn't pay its writers the highest rates, it was one of the few markets at the time for supernatural fiction, thus attracting writers who specialized in that genre who couldn't sell their work elsewhere.

The condition of this issue is as follows. The front cover has some minor chips and tears, but colors are still bright and the magazine displays well. The interior is in generally average condition for its age, fairly sound with typical browning of pages and some brittleness. Unfortunately, the back cover and the last few pages are missing. However, since Stephen's objective was to find a copy of August Simpson's story THE BOOK OF SHADOWS (which is still intact) the defects in this issue actually work to his advantage. Normally, if I had a copy of this issue for sale in very good or better condition, I'd charge $500 - $750 for it. But, given the fact it is missing several pages, I'm asking only $175. I feel the price is very reasonable. I'm only aware of two other copies of this particular issue that have come on the market in the last ten years and they are now in private collections.

Please pass this news on to Stephen and ask him to call me as soon as possible.

Sincerely,

Glenn Goggin

## Clark, Margaret

**From:** dastern@mac.com
**Sent:** Friday, January 28, 2000 15:40:56 AM
**To:** Clark, Margaret
**Subject:** Blair Witch: Hysteria or History

Wow. How are we going to make a book out of that?

# THE BOSTON TIMES

# Stephen and Tristen:

The race to map the human genome takes an unexpected detour • Matthew Jordan Bugs Bunny, Bart Simpson, and...Bad Elves? • Craig Kaffafian

They wrote themselves a storybook romance...right up until the last chapter • Howard Kornheiser

Re-imagining Downtown: An architect's roundtable

# If fairy tales can come true...
# Can nightmares too?

## Dream Lovers

Howard Kornheiser

It seeps through the cobblestoned streets, wafts from the perpetually burning gaslights, peers out from the shuttered windows of block after block of brick-faced row houses. You can feel it standing on the steps of the Old South Meeting House, site of a 1774 public meeting that turned into the infamous Boston Tea Party, or sitting on the stools lining the bar of the Bull & Finch pub, whose exterior is seen on *Cheers*. You can find it, in fact, just about everywhere you go within this mile-square enclave of downtown Boston bounded by Beacon, Bowdoin, and Cambridge streets and Storrow Drive.

"It" is tradition, and there is no place on Earth more devoted to maintaining "it" than the neighborhood known as Beacon Hill.

And there is no part of Beacon Hill more steeped in history than its South Slope, home since the late 1700s to the crème de la crème of Boston society. The Boston Brahmins, whose members included the physician and humorist Oliver Wendell Holmes, the prominent clergyman Daniel Howe, and lawyer Barclay Parker, all resided in Beacon Hill.

Parker's family, in fact, still maintains a home on the South Slope, though the family's primary residence is now in Brookline. His descendants have also maintained their standing in Boston's legal community: great-great grandson William Parker was a founding member of Parker, Slate, White, and Bedrum, one of the city's largest and most prestigious firms. William's eldest son, Sanford, now a junior partner at his father's firm, has ensured that tradition will live on for at least another generation. Middle son Lucas has also honored the family legacy by setting up shop as in-house counsel for Bendickson-Gambel, a prestigious Washington, D.C., securities firm.

And then there's William's youngest child, Stephen, who began rejecting the family tradition at the age of 18: first, by attending Yale University (brothers, father, and grandfather all matriculated at Harvard) and second, by choosing a career as a historian. Heretical though his behavior may have seemed at the time, however, it pales when placed beside Stephen's actions of

September, actions that resulted in his becoming the first member in his family's august history to be charged with murder.

Beacon Hill has the history, but Boston's oldest buildings, to the surprise of many visitors, are to be found in the outlying community of Dorchester. The William Blake House (c. 1650) is, in fact, one of the oldest surviving structures in all of New England. Although Dorchester has a rich colonial tradition, however today it is one of the most ethnically and financially diverse suburbs in New England.

The grand Victorian homes on Harley Avenue stand on the border between the two: in early 1977, a young couple named George and Irene Ryler, both teachers, purchased one of those homes and set about simultaneously renovating it and beginning a family. Their first child, Tristen, was born in 1978; younger sister Suzanne followed two years later.

Work on the house, George recalls, took somewhat longer to get going.

"We lived for five years without a dining room table. Two without a door on our bedroom. And six without a bathtub." He

laughs, and for a moment, the deep circles under his eyes and the numbness etched on his face disappear. "Lots of baths in the kitchen sink for the kids."

The house on Harley Avenue is an imposing showplace now, but peering out from around every corner are memories of the never-ending home renovation project it used to be, and the family that lived there. George, a stocky, fair-haired man in his early fifties, spent almost every summer stripping wallpaper, painting and scraping woodwork, sanding and polishing floors. Every square inch of the house contains his blood and sweat. When he and Irene purchased the home 23 years ago, they planned to live in it forever.

Early last week, they put it on the market.

"We want to be gone by Christmas," said Irene. She and George have already resigned their positions at Dorchester High. Their younger daughter, Suzanne, is attending school in Atlanta; they plan to seek work there. Even if they don't find work right away, the money from the sale of their home will be more than enough to keep them comfortable...though comfortable is, perhaps, the wrong word to use. Comfort is not something George and Irene Ryler expect to find for a long time.

"I keep asking myself if there was a reason for what he did to my little girl," Irene says. "I wake up at night, wanting to know why."

George Ryler is a little more blunt in his choice of words. "I don't need to know why," he says. "I just need five minutes alone with that bastard."

Although William Parker was angered by his son's choice of career and school, it caused no permanent rift between the two. Rather the opposite, according to some: Stephen, in carving his own path, won his father's respect in a way that neither of his two older brothers had. But in summer 1995, that respect turned once again to disappointment when Stephen skipped out on the Parker family reunion (an event some five years in the planning), deciding instead to tour Europe with his girlfriend. That year of travel turned into a year of writing and research, which, though it cost him the girlfriend, eventually resulted in his first book, *Beyond the Pale: The Extraordinary Life of Daniel Douglas Home.* Published by Yale University Press in 1998, it won Stephen the prestigious Lomax Fellowship, which carried with it a cash award that strengthened his independence from his family.

In the fall of 1996, however, the book's primary effect on his life was not financial. Rather, *Beyond the Pale* sparked an interest on Stephen's part in the history of supernatural beliefs, and though Yale did not normally provide for graduate work in that area, Stephen's preliminary work on the book persuaded Armand Soltzmann, a professor in the religion department, to sponsor his proposed dissertation. In September, Stephen returned to Yale and began his academic career as a graduate student, which brought with it a whole new set of responsibilities, one of which was serving as a teaching assistant to Professor Soltzmann for his large lecture courses.

Almost exactly two years earlier, another college student had also decided to make the supernatural the focus of her work. In April 1994, Heather Donahue, then in her last year at Montgomery Community College in Rockville, Maryland, put together a proposal for a short documentary she felt sure would be her entree into the upper echelon of filmmaking schools. The subject of her film: a little-known (at the time) piece of local folklore, the Blair Witch. Her professor was equally enthusiastic about the potential of Heather's film, and by the fall of that year, she had managed to beg, borrow, and otherwise wrangle the equipment she needed to turn her dream into reality. On October 20, 1994, Heather Donahue, Joshua Leonard, and Michael Williams began filming her thesis in the town of Burkittsville, Maryland. A day later, they set off into the woods surrounding the town to film some of the sites associated with the legend of the Blair Witch.

The three were never seen again.

While the Ryler home may have been shy a door or a coat of paint from time to time, books were never in short supply. Tristen learned to read at an early age, and, by the time she was in grade school, was making up her own stories, most of them centering around the adventures of a close-knit group of teenage girls.

"It was like the *Baby-Sitters Club*, only it was about Tris and her friends," remembers sister Suzanne, from her Atlanta dormitory. After three years spent in the deep South, traces of a southern drawl have slipped into the Ryler's younger daughter's speech. That drawl, however, disappears each time the conversation turns to her older sister.

"I remember begging her and begging her to put me into one of those stories. God, how she must have hated that!" Tristen eventually gave in, and wrote her younger sister into a children's story called "The Little Girl from Planet Stein." That piece won the elder Ryler sister the first of several literary prizes during her high school years (another prize brought her to Washington, D.C., for lunch at the White House). Those honors, coupled with a perfect score on the English portion of her SATs, garnered Tristen both a scholarship and a spot in Yale University's freshman class of 1996.

That first year, her class schedule reflected her wide-ranging interests and her already-evident bent toward writing. Included among her spring semester choices was Introduction to World Religion, a lecture course given by Professor Armand Soltzmann. According to school records, 121 of Tristen's freshman classmates also took the class. As is typical of courses with such large numbers of students, Soltzmann prepared and delivered the lectures and handed out assignments, but he depended on a complement of graduate students to help him grade the large volume of papers and to tutor students; among his assistants that semester was Stephen Ryan Parker.

Ryler and Parker hit it off immediately, and by the middle of that semester, Tristen had broken up with her high school boyfriend and moved into Stephen's Wooster Street apartment. The two, according to friends, were inseparable.

A few years later, Stephen's professional career was also on the upswing. Having proven his ability to stand on his own two feet, he left Yale in 1999 and returned to Boston, taking an apartment in the heart of Cambridge. The family welcomed him back with open arms, a welcome that extended to his new girlfriend Ryler.

The two quickly made themselves at home in their new neighborhood. Right downstairs was Java Joe's, where they spent virtually every morning huddled over an array of baked goods, caffeinated beverages, and newspapers. Down the block was Mughlai Palace, a n Indian restaurant where the staff remembers the two having many cozy late-night dinners. And if they wanted entertainment, just around the corner were a movie theater, a blues club, and a playhouse. Cambridge, it seemed to them, had everything.

On the evening of July 16 Stephen and Tristen, having spent the day working in their apartment, decided to treat themselves to a film. But when they arrived at the Kendall Square Cinema, they found a line of eager ticket-holders already circling the block. The show they were hoping to see was long sold out, as were all shows for that night, and the next. Everyone in town, it seemed, was a step ahead of them in discovering the surprise blockbuster that would prove to be summer's hottest ticket: *The Blair Witch Project*, Heather Donahue's rescued and restored film thesis. In the weeks to come, that film would go on to captivate the nation.

It was the hysteria surrounding it, however, that sparked Stephen's interest.

Over the next two weeks, he began shaping his impressions of that hysteria into a book proposal, setting aside a collection of essays on which he had begun work. By the end of July, he'd put together an extended outline for *Witchhunt: The Search for Elly Kedward*, and sent it on to his agent. That proposal, however, came flying back almost as quickly as it had gone out.

"The problem with *Witchhunt* wasn't the topic. It was the execution." So says agent Jennifer Gates, talking from her New York City office. "He'd come up with this great concept, and proceeded to drown it in endless layers of historical detail. He lost the heart of the idea."

The rejection, according to friends, hit Stephen hard. Understandably—this was his first taste of failure. Gates, however, took care to stress that the problems were, in her mind, eminently fixable. "I asked him to take out some of the historical detail, and make it a little more user-friendly. I told him I thought the project was very timely, and very saleable, with some fine-tuning."

Enter Tristen Ryler.

While Stephen had no desire to revisit the scene of his failure, she immediately grasped what Gates had been trying to tell her boyfriend. What happened next is a matter of some dispute.

"Tris took his idea, and reworked it," says Suzanne Ryler's sister. "She made it into a book that could sell, and that made him angry. That's when their problems started. That's what she told me."

"As I understand it," says Turner's close friend, writer John Usler, "Tristen simply encouraged Stephen himself to revisit the proposal. While she may have helped him shape it, the writing itself was almost exclusively his."

Gates herself doesn't know how the

**Stephen Ryan Parker. (Courtesy Lucas Parker)**

**Tristen Ryler. (Courtesy George and Irene Ryler)**

new proposal took shape, only that by the middle of August, she had an outline for *The Blair Witch: Hysteria or History?* in her hands. The material went out to a select group of New York publishers, and quickly sold to Pocket Books, a division of Simon & Schuster, for a respectable sum "in the high five figures."

That sale, according to friends, is when the trouble began.

"It would be premature to divulge our defense strategy at this time." To date, those words are the sum total of public statements issuing from the team of lawyers handling Stephen's case. Lead counsel for the five-man group is a short, balding man named Karl Immerhauser. Although Immerhauser and company lack the star power of O.J. Simpson's "dream team," they have among them more than a century of trial experience.

Prosecuting the case is Jake Holt, Frederick County district attorney, who has been more forthcoming regarding his trial tactics. The heart of the prosecution's case is a videotape they plan to screen for the jury. It captures in graphic detail the murder of Tristen Ryler, at the unforgiving hands of her boyfriend and cowriter, Stephen Ryan Parker.

The relationship between Tristen and Stephen may have begun to unravel with the sale of their book. It certainly was strained by the beginning of September; the late-night dinners at Mughlai Palace turned from cozy to confrontational, and the two often spent days at a time working apart. Tristen spent more than one evening dining with her parents at their Dorchester home, occasions Irene Ryler remembers were colored by her daughter's sullen, angry mood. Wednesday night, September 8, was one such meal: turkey burgers, carrot slaw, and monosyllabic slabs of conversation.

"I knew something was wrong then," says her mother. "I wish to God I'd made her talk to me about it."

It was the last time George and Irene Ryler saw their daughter alive.

On September 10 Stephen Ryan Parker and Tristen Ryler left for a wedding in Minnesota. They spent a weekend, relaxing with friends, after which Stephen continued on to a conference in San Diego and Tristen returned to their Cambridge home. On September 20 they were together again, bound for Burkittsville, Maryland.

The details of that trip are now supermarket tabloid fodder, as are the grisly photos that chronicled them. Of all the tragedies that occurred that weekend, however, the one that surprised George and Irene Ryler the most is the one that has made the least news: the miscarriage suffered by their eldest daughter the day before her murder. Tristen, they were shocked to learn, was six weeks pregnant with Stephen's child.

Phone records the day before her trip to Burkittsville show Tristen placing a call to the Daniel Brighton Family Planning Clinic in Cambridge. What she talked about remains private, but it seems a fair bet to suggest that terminating the pregnancy was a topic of conversation. Indeed, according to her closest friends—including sister Suzanne—having children was not an item high on Tristen's current agenda. On the other hand, Stephen, say those same people, was ready to begin a family. Those conflicting desires erupted during their trip to Burkittsville, resulting in Tristen's death.

The issue, however, may not be as cut-and-dried as all that.

The evidence incriminating Stephen Ryan Parker, Kim Diamond, and Jeff Patterson for their roles in what has come to be known as "The Black Hills Murders" was discovered by police in Patterson's loft in Jericho Mills, a small town outside of Burkittsville. Along with the videotape mentioned above, as well as another supposedly incriminating Patterson in the murder of nineteen-year-old Erica Geerson, police found a number of files with Patterson's writing on them, files that contained personal documents relating to Parker, Ryler, Diamond, and Geerson.

"We don't know where he got this material," said Burkittsville Sheriff Ronald Cravens. "Or how, for that matter."

That material purportedly includes a diary kept by Ryler for the past three months, one that Parker's defense attorneys are anxious to get their hands on. According to sources, that diary paints the relationship between their client and Tristen Ryler in a far more positive light than the evidence that has surfaced to date. None of that matters to the murdered girl's father.

"I didn't see the tape. I haven't seen the diary," George Ryler says. "I didn't see *The Blair Witch Project*, either. What I saw was my little girl, put in a wooden box and lowered into the ground. It's as simple as that."

## Clark, Margaret

Yeah, those files, the ones that Craven was talking about. Good idea.

Burkittsville, here I come.

Blue Files

STEPHEN RYAN PARKER

Patterson

TRISTEN RYLER

ERICA GEERSON

KIM DIAMOND

KIM DIAMOND

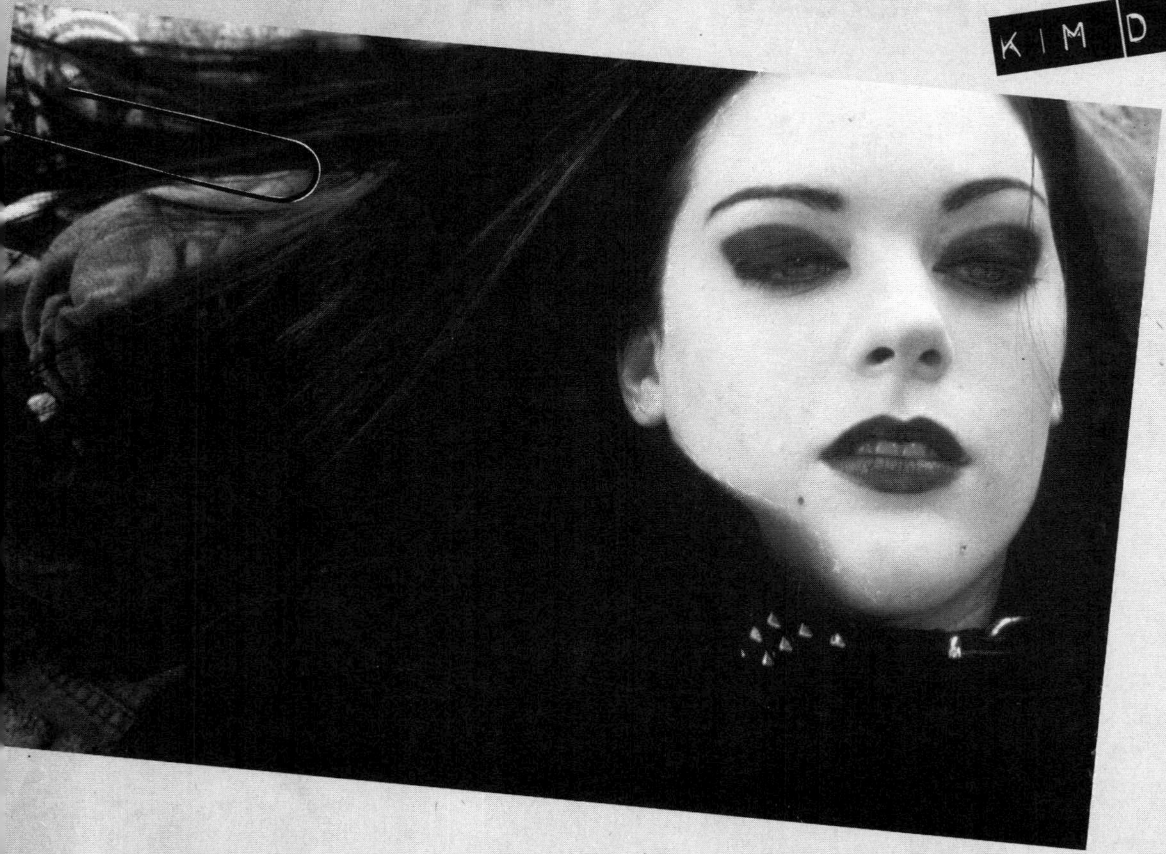

# Three Teens Caught in Spray-Paint Spree

by Laurie Smith
Staff Reporter

Three area teens were arrested shortly after one a.m. last night after a brief chase by police through city streets. They were identified as Marie Parsons, 16, and Linda Hunter, 16, of Aurora, and Kim Diamond, 15, of Sugar Grove. The three were spotted by a patrol car defacing numerous storefronts along Main Street. Police booked them on charges of criminal mischief, trespassing, and malicious destruction of property.

The arrest is the first for Parsons and Hunter: Diamond has previously been arraigned on petty theft charges.

## CAMP LAGAUGE

**REFERRAL FORM**

**Date:** April 13, 1994

**Child's Name:** Kimberly Lynn Diamond
**Address:** 461 1/2 Main Street
Sugar Grove IL 63780
**Child's Age:** 15
**Child's Criminal Record:** petty theft, criminal mischief
**Child's Legal Guardian:** Brazzio Diamond
**Referring Agency:** Kane County Family Services
**Sponsoring Agent:** Ellen Sherk

**Comments:**

Kimberly is a strong-willed girl of above-average intelligence whose performance in the classroom and outside school is not indicative of her potential. She has been cited for truancy on numerous occasions over the past year.

I have been counseling Kimberly for almost a year, during which time I have heard very disturbing reports about her home living situation. I have been unable to schedule a single meeting with Kimberly's father and step-mother to discuss her situation. Regardless, I believe her home life be one that is not supportive of her expressed desires to change her pattern of behavior.

I believe time in a more structured environment such as Camp LaGuage would do Kimberly a world of good.

# INCIDENT REPORT

**Date:** November 16, 1994

**Supervisor:** Robert Earlington

**Location:** cafeteria

**Participants:** Kimberly Diamond, Anthony Chen, Anne
Mainberger, Chantay Hughes

## Details of Incident:

I was supervising Diamond, Chen, Mainberger, and Hughes
on cafeteria clean-up duty. Diamond, Chen, and Hughes were
working in one room, I was with Mainberger in another. I
first heard the sounds of shouting, and then a fight.

I went into the dining room and found Hughes trying
to attack Diamond with a kitchen knife. Chen was holding
her back.

Chen later told me Diamond provoked the fight by
taunting Hughes.

## Action taken:

Off-camp privileges suspended for Diamond: warnings
inserted in Hughes' file. No action taken against Chen.

# INCIDENT REPORT

**Date:** November 17, 1994

**Supervisor:** Robert Earlington

**Location:** Maintenance Building

**Participants:** Kimberly Diamond, Chantay Hughes

## Details of Incident:

Diamond and Hughes were discovered fighting with each other shortly after breakfast this morning. When I arrived, Hughes had Diamond in a choke hold and was hitting her in the face, saying "you couldn't have known that" repeatedly. Neither girl would elaborate on the incident further.

## Action taken:

Off-camp privileges suspended for Hughes: this was the third incident involving Diamond in the last two months, resulting in her automatic expulsion from the camp.

## REFERRAL FORM

**Date:** June 14, 1995

**Child's Name:** Kim Diamond
**Address:** 1336 Newland Ave.
Chicago IL 60643
**Child's Age:** 16
**Child's Criminal Record:** petty theft, criminal mischief
**Child's Legal Guardian:** Brazzio Diamond
**Referring Agency:** Kane County Family Services
**Sponsoring Agent:** Ellen Sherk

**Comments:**

In the six months since her previous expulsion from Camp LaGauge, Kim has refrained from engaging in any further disruptive activities. She has moved away from her disruptive home environment, which has greatly helped her overall outlook on life. At the same time, I do not feel her current group living situation is ultimately any healthier for her.

I have discussed the possibility of returning to Camp LaGauge with her, and she seems enthusiastic about the idea.

# INCIDENT REPORT

**Date:** August 26, 1995

**Supervisor:** Robert Earlington

**Location:** cafeteria

**Participants:** Kim Diamond, Anne Mainberger

## Details of Incident:

Diamond was being verbally abusive to Mainberger, at which point I intervened. During our subsequent argument, she revealed personal details concerning this employee which could only have been obtained through the misappropriation of confidential camp records.

## Action taken:

As per the terms of her readmittance to the camp, permanent expulsion.

# INCIDENT REPORT . .

**Date:** August 27, 1995

**Supervisor:** Robert Earlington

**Location:** Administration Building

**Participants:** Kim Diamond

## Details of Incident:
This morning the words "Nothing Matters and What if It Did" were spray-painted across the building. This phrase is one Diamond has been repeating througout her latest stay at the Camp.

**Action taken:** None necessary.

# THE BLAIR WITCH HUNT
**Tour Questionnaire**

Thank you for your interest in The Blair Witch Hunt.
Our tour provides you with an up-close look at all the sites
made famous in the Blair Witch Project, as well as many others
haunted by the famous Blair Witch.

In order to make your journey as satisfying as possible, we
need to ask you a few short questions.

**Name** Kim Diamond
**Address** 1336 Newland Ave.
**City, State, Zip** Chicago IL 60643
**Phone**
**Fax**
**E-mail** gothgrrl @ coolmail.com
**Age** 22
**Occupation** Genius
**Method of payment:**
[ ] Visa
[ ] MasterCard
[X] Check
**Card #**
**Expiration Date**

**Select the sites that most interest you:**

[X] Burkittsville Union Cemetery
[X] Rustin Parr's House
[X] Coffin Rock
[X] Burkittsville Courthouse
[X] Tappy East Creek
[X] The Old Brody House
[X] Nanticoke Graveyard

**Are there any other sites related to the Blair Witch you would like to see?**

The Blair Witch Cult

**Would you be interested in a tour of the area's historic Civil War sites, including Antietam, American National Battlefield, and historic Burkittsville?**
[ ]Yes
[X]No

**Are you interested in an overnight, or day trip?**
[X]Overnight
[ ] Day

**Sleeping bags and tents are available for rental to all overnight tour guests at a nominal cost: you can supply your own, if desired.**
[ ] I plan to bring my own camping gear
I need to rent a
[ ] Sleeping bag          *what's a tent?*
[ ] Tent

**Meals are included in the cost of your trip. Please list any special dietary requirements in the space below:**

beer

**Any other comments?**

what do we hunt with? should I bring a gun?

RESET

Tour group size is limited to six people: groups are matched according to age and interest. We encourage individuals to become acquainted prior to tour date.

[X] Share my information with other tour members
[ ] Do not share my information with other tour members

You can either submit this form on-line, along with your credit card number to guarantee your reservation (we use secure SSL servers, so have no fear ), or print the complete form out and mail with either a credit card number or your $50 deposit to:

**THE BLAIR WITCH HUNT**
RFD 431, Rural Route 4
Jericho Mills, MD 36361

**From:** **gothgrrrl@coolmail.com**
To: witchfinder@netfree.org
**Subject:Blair Witch Hunt**
Date: Thursday, September 16, 1999 17:11:16 AM

I don't understand how the check could have bounced. Here's my credit card info (the card belongs to Lauren Goddard, who's my stepmother).

VISA ###########0644
Expiration Date 4/03

I am driving with friends as far east as Pittsburgh: after that, I will be making my way toward Burkittsville by hook, crook, or whatever other means necessary.

I'll e-mail you from the road.

ERICA GEERSON

# THE BLAIR WITCH HUNT
**Tour Questionnaire**

Thank you for your interest in The Blair Witch Hunt.
Our tour provides you with an up-close look at all the sites
made famous in the Blair Witch Project, as well as many others
haunted by the famous Blair Witch.

In order to make your journey as satisfying as possible, we
need to ask you a few short questions.

**Name** Erica Geerson
**Address** 22 Jurgens Drive
**City, State, Zip** Munnsville IL 40443
**Phone**
**Fax**
**E-mail** wiccan2@munns.edu.org
**Age** 19
**Occupation** Student
**Method of payment:**
[X] **Visa**
[ ] **MasterCard**
[ ] **Check**
**Card #** XXXXXXXXXX
**Expiration Date** XXXX

**Select the sites that most interest you:**

[ ] **Burkittsville Union Cemetery**
[X] **Rustin Parr's House**
[ ] **Coffin Rock**
[ ] **Burkittsville Courthouse**
[ ] **Tappy East Creek**
[ ] **The Old Brody House**
[ ] **Nanticoke Graveyard**

**Are there any other sites related to the Blair Witch you would like to see?**

```
Sites related to Elly Kedward:
location of her house? Grave?
```

**Would you be interested in a tour of the area's historic Civil War sites, including Antietam, American National Battlefield, and historic Burkittsville?**
[ ] Yes
[x] No

**Are you interested in an overnight, or day trip?**
[x] Overnight
[ ] Day

**Sleeping bags and tents are available for rental to all overnight tour guests at a nominal cost: you can supply your own, if desired.**
[ ] I plan to bring my own camping gear
I need to rent a
[x] Sleeping bag
[x] Tent

**Meals are included in the cost of your trip. Please list any special dietary requirements in the space below:**

```
I am a vegetarian
```

**Any other comments?**

RESET

Tour group size is limited to six people: groups are matched according to age and interest. We encourage individuals to become acquainted prior to tour date.

[ ] Share my information with other tour members
[x] Do not share my information with other tour members

You can either submit this form on-line, along with your credit card number to guarantee your reservation (we use secure SSL servers, so have no fear ), or print the complete form out and mail with either a credit card number or your $50 deposit to:

**THE BLAIR WITCH HUNT**
**RFD 431, Rural Route 4**
**Jericho Mills, MD 36361**

**Inbox**

From:    witchfinder@netfree.org
To:       wiccan2@munns.edu.org
Subject: Hello?
Date:    Sunday, September 12, 1999

Erica Geerson, are you out there? I sent you a brochure in the mail: it just came back marked "Return to Sender. Address Unknown."

Inbox

9/18/99 5:11

**Inbox**

From:    **wicccan2@munns.edu.org**
To:      witchfinder@netfree.org
Subject: **Hello?**
Date:    Sunday, September 12, 1999 17:11:16 AM

Here I am.
After ten tomorrow night, I'll be in the Wicca chatroom at coolmail.com.

**Participants**

witchfinder
elodie
agnes
dianea
arthur
corinne
mistressA
elizabethm

**agnes:** that's how it is with daughters

**elizabethm:** agreed. i have the same problem with mine

**witchfinder:** hello

**dianea:** welcome...Witchfinder?

**witchfinder:** hello. is one of you erica?

**mistressA:** no there's no Erica here

**elodie:** where are you from witchfinder?

**witchfinder:** Maryland

**agnes:** you're not one of those Blair Witch people, are you? They've really made a mess of things for us.

**elizabethm:** please let's not start all that again

**wiccan2:** hello jeff

**witchfinder:** erica

**wiccan2:** yeah

**witchfinder:** cool. you're all set for the tour on the 20th

**wiccan2:** okay

**witchfinder:** hey in the questionnaire you said you wanted to know more about Elly Kedward you should plan on stopping in Baltimore at the Maryland Historical Society they have a copy of a novel this guy wrote back in like 1800 about Elly

**wiccan2:**  the Blair Witch Cult

**witchfinder:** that's right

**wiccan2:** what makes you think it's a novel?

**witchfinder:** ha ha

**wiccan2:** I'm serious

**witchfinder:** you've read it?

**wiccan2:** yeah i have

**witchfinder:** and you think that stuff really happened that way?

**wiccan2:** some of it is the truth, I believe.

**witchfinder:** PUH-LEAZE!!!

**wiccan2:** Seriously. Elly Kedward was a victim: just like those children.

**witchfinder:** don't go spreading that around when you get here. it won't make you too popular.

**wiccan2:** don't worry. I'm not crazy. Nobody's going to have to worry about me kidnapping children.

**witchfinder:** what's that supposed to mean?

**witchfinder:** erica?

**elodie:** witchfinder? are you still there?

**witchfinder:** sure

**elodie:** something was weird on my computer for a second

**elizabethm:** mine too

**witchfinder:** erica?

**agnes:** there's no Erica here, and please tell us your name so we don't have to keep calling you witchfinder. it has unpleasant connotations.

**elizabethm:** witchfinder?

**agnes:** gone. logged out.

# COMPOSITION BOOK

100 SHEETS • 9 3/4 in. x 7 1/2 in.

TRISTEN RYLER

**Pen-Tab**

**Pen-Tab Industries, Inc.**
Front Royal, VA 22630
*Virginia • Kansas City • Los Angeles*

50105

# THE BLAIR WITCH HUNT
## Tour Questionnaire

Thank you for your interest in The Blair Witch Hunt.
Our tour provides you with an up-close look at all the sites
made famous in the Blair Witch Project, as well as many others
haunted by the famous Blair Witch.

In order to make your journey as satisfying as possible, we
need to ask you a few short questions.

**Name** Tristan Ryler
**Address** 313 kendall common Building 85
**City, State, Zip** cambridge MA 02141
**Phone** 617 555 9321
**Fax** 617 555 9321
**E-mail** Ryler1979@coolmail.com
**Age** 22
**Occupation** writer
**Method of payment:**
[x] Visa
[ ] MasterCard
[ ] Check
**Card #** X
**Expiration Date** X

**Select the sites that most interest you:**

[ ] Burkittsville Union Cemetery
[x] Rustin Parr's House
[x] Coffin Rock
[ ] Burkittsville Courthouse
[x] Tappy East Creek
[ ] The Old Brody House
[ ] Nanticoke Graveyard

**Are there any other sites related to the Blair Witch you would like to see?**

creegan's loft?

**Would you be interested in a tour of the area's historic Civil War sites, including Antietam, American National Battlefield, and historic Burkittsville?**
[X] Yes
[ ] No

**Are you interested in an overnight, or day trip?**
[X] Overnight
[ ] Day

**Sleeping bags and tents are available for rental to all overnight tour guests at a nominal cost: you can supply your own, if desired.**
[ ] I plan to bring my own camping gear
I need to rent a
[X] Sleeping bag
[X] Tent

**Meals are included in the cost of your trip. Please list any special dietary requirements in the space below:**

**Any other comments?**

RESET

Tour group size is limited to six people: groups are matched according to age and interest. We encourage individuals to become acquainted prior to tour date.

[X] Share my information with other tour members
[ ] Do not share my information with other tour members

You can either submit this form on-line, along with your credit card number to guarantee your reservation (we use secure SSL servers, so have no fear ), or print the complete form out and mail with either a credit card number or your $50 deposit to:

**THE BLAIR WITCH HUNT**
**RFD 431, Rural Route 4**
**Jericho Mills, MD 36361**

September 4

Morning pages again.

NO: now these are my mourning pages.

Oh my GOD. What am I going to do? Sit at home, and change diapers? No fucking way. But who else is going to do it. He's got another book contract, he's got a conference coming up, he's got to bring home the bacon, so he can't do it. Just being practical, honey. Mr. practical, Mr. cynical, Mr. if you can't film it, it didn't happen. Who's a better writer? Who's a better journalist? Who's going in with an open mind, and who wants to classify everything according to pre-existing categories of supernatural?

Who's got the award? Who's the freshman who slept with her t.a.?

Fuck me, fuck me, fuck me: what was I thinking?

There. I feel better now.

Okay. Now back to life as we know it.

I have to set up lunch with Margaret the next time I'm in New York to talk about the novel idea. Which means I have to get the shit out of my head and on paper. I don't know why anybody hasn't thought of this before, to do a historical novel based on the Blair Witch events, kind of a Jayne Anne Krentz or Linda Howard take on it. I could do that: the problem is finding a protagonist. Robin Weaver is a good possibility: she lived till sometime in the fifties, I think, so she was around for Parr.

Pain in my ass, I've only been spending about five minutes each morning on these pages anyway and now Stephen's up and already in the shower and that means I don't even get that much today. ARGGGGHHH!

September 5

Blair witch jokes:

What's black and white and red all over?

Rustin Parr's diary

What were Heather's last words?

Cut!

What were Mike's last words?

Cut! Cut!

What were Josh's last words?

It's hard to talk without your teeth.

Why did the little girl cross Black Rock Road?

Wait, wait, wait...

Serious sick joke:

There's something growing inside me.

Gotta talk to somebody: Marion's at work, Alison's off in France, Suzanne would be too excited to talk rationally, and Mom...

Mom would want to know when the wedding was.

So what's wrong with a wedding?

Stephen is highly kid-friendly.

Stephen's family is highly kid-friendly.

Stephen's family is good people, especially Lucas and Darcy.

When he isn't being a pompous know-it-all, Stephen is the most wonderful guy I've ever met in my life and I so love him though I wish sometimes he was a little more...adventurous.

I better hope he never finds this, or he'll kill me.

Okay...enough navel-gazing.

The novel:

I've decided the historical Elly has to be a central figure, because that's where the curse all started. With those little kids, in the woods. The problem is I don't want to do a multi-generational eight hundred page thing, I want one central protagonist who is both affected by the curse and directly involved in it. Actually, now that I think about it, I wonder about picking one of the kids from the late 1700s. A girl who survived right up until the Coffin Rock incident...though that still misses out on Rustin Parr. Though I suppose I could end with her living long enough to meet a very young Parr at the end of the book. Maybe the kid is the witch? NO: how about the kid was a friend of Elly's, she finds Elly's spellbook after Elly is killed, and casts a spell cursing the kids who killed Elly. Hey, yeah, and part of the deal is their deaths are the price the kid pays for immortality?

Hmmm.

September 6

Shit.

I had just about decided to do the novel from Robin Weaver's persepective, when I went back through Wood Witch Said and realized Malvey already wrote about it that way.

That did give me some ideas about Eileen Treacle, though.

1) Her body was never recovered

2) So what if... she didn't die, but became the witch's apprentice, too?

3) What happened to the town as a result of her drowning? I mean, historically. The whole thing about the bundles of sticks, and the river getting oily, that seems pretty far-out. Calls for a trip to the library.

Which luckily is on my agenda for today. Speaking of which...

Why do I always have to go to the library and xerox the newspaper articles, the magazine pieces, the stuff that a third-grader could do? Why is it me calling up the old stoned hippies and crawling through clouds of smoke to get a copy of Creegan's stupid-ass manifesto anyway? I'm tired of it. When are they going to put all this shit on the Internet anyway?

Deep breath, Tris.

# OUR PRINCIPLES:
## ALL WHO SHARE THEM, ARE WELCOME TO SHARE OUR SPACE

All of us, red and black, yellow and white, man and woman, young and old, are human beings.

WE TREAT EACH OTHER WITH RESPECT.

The earth is our mother: she was here long before us, and will be long after.

WE TREAT THE EARTH WITH RESPECT.

Nature is the god we worship: her power is mysterious, and awe-inspiring.

WE TREAT NATURE'S POWER WITH RESPECT.

Words have power: we do not use them hurtfully, or lightly.

WE TREAT THE MYSTERY OF LANGUAGE WITH RESPECT.

Human beings are sexual creatures: the act of sex is our reason for being, and our natural duty.

WE TREAT THE ACT OF SEX WITH RESPECT.

Money is not an end, but a means to an end.

Drugs are not an end, but a means to an end.

Power is not an end, but a means to an end.

Our goal is enlightenment of the mind.

Our goal is fulfillment of the spirit.

Our goal is transcendence of the physical.

STEPHEN RYAN PARKER

## Inbox

**From:** lomaxfellow@coolmail.com
To:      witchfinder@netfree.org
**Subject:Blair Witch: Hysteria or History**
Date:    Sunday, September 12, 1999 13:04:53 PM

Jeff-

Hope you don't mind, but I didn't fill out the questionnaire. My answers would be pretty much the same as Tristen's, anyway.

As I said on the phone, our book is as much about the phenomenon of "mass hysteria" as it is about the Blair Witch (we talk about other historical examples as well, Area 51 and Bigfoot from this country, the Loch Ness Monster and Bloody Sam Caine from England). In that regard, we're hoping we can spend a little time with you talking about your experiences in Burkittsville during the whole Blair Witch Project phenomenon.

We're both looking forward to the tour next month.


Thanks.

**Inbox**

From:     witchfinder@netfree.org
To:       lomaxfellow@coolmail.com
Subject:  Re: Blair Witch Hysteriaor History
Date:     Sunday, September 12, 1999

Can't help you with Heather, Josh, and Mike: I wasn't around for that.
I was out in the woods last week, though and saw Elvis, if that's any
help.

Jeff

P.S. — Seriously... Bloddy Sam, huh? My dad used to tell me stories
about that guy.

**From:** **lomaxfellow@coolmail.com**
To:      witchfinder@netfree.org
**Subject:Bloody Sam Stories**
Date:    Monday, September 13, 1999 8:12:15 AM

Like this one?

We were going to put it in our book, but the editor nixed it.

# Fairy Tales and Folklore
of
# Lancashire County

*Retold by Robert Stockwell*

# Bloody Sam of Malkin Tower

At the edge of Pendle Forest lived a farmer, his wife, and their two sons. They were poor folk, and even in good times had barely enough food to go around. When a plague came upon their crops, they had nothing to trade at market. Each day they had less and less to eat, and always the parents gave their two boys the largest part of what food there was.

One night, the elder boy, Robert, spoke to his brother, Jamie, as they lay in bed.

"Father is skin and bones," said he.

"And Mother is starving," said Jamie.

"We are of age to be apprenticed," said Rob. "Now we must find our own way in the world, or watch our parents die of hunger before our eyes."

They resolved to leave home the next morning. Yet the thought of leaving behind the place they had lived all their lives and the parents who loved them was hard. Jamie cried himself to sleep that night, and Rob stayed awake until the dawn.

Still, as the sun arose, the boys gathered their courage and left. They followed the trail into Pendle Forest, but as day wore on the path vanished and the boys soon were quite lost. As night fell, they came upon an old and crumbling tower in the wood. It looked abandoned, yet smoke rose from the top of it.

"Perhaps we can find shelter for the night here," said Rob. So, summoning up his courage, he knocked upon the door.

"Who goes there?" came a voice. "Robert and James Rowland, both of us able-bodied boys willing to work for our supper."

"Boys?" said the voice, and then the door opened, and standing before them was a giant of a man, with one good leg and one he dragged behind him. He was so ugly that despite the lure of the warm fire within, Rob and Jamie were both anxious to leave.

"Enter, and fear not," said he, crooking a finger at them. "My fire is warm and I have food to share."

At the mention of food, the boys quite forgot their fears, for they had eaten nothing all day save two or three berries they had found on the ground.

They entered and the man set them places at his table.

"What are your names?" he asked.

"I am Robert Rowland."

"And I am Jamie Rowland. We have run away from our home because there was not enough food to go around for all."

"Such good boys," said the man. "You need go hungry no longer."

So saying, he ladled them out some stew from his pot. While they ate, Rob looked around the room. He was surprised to see a great black crow perched above the fireplace.

"That is my pet, of sorts," said the man, noticing his gaze. "A well-behaved bird is he."

When the two boys were stuffed full and could eat no more, the man showed them to two pretty little beds covered in white linen, and Rob and Jamie lay down in them, and thought they were in heaven.

But the man was only pretending to be kind, for he was in truth Bloody Sam, the murderer of Lancashire Castle, who lay in wait for children. When one fell within his power, he killed it, cooked it until the child was juicy, and ate it. Then he used the child's bones and blood to perform his wicked magic. He had seen the boys coming toward him from high atop the tower, and had planned their fates from that moment.

Now he watched Jamie and Robert sleeping, and thought to himself, "either one, once fattened up, will make a dainty mouthful, but the younger the child, the sweeter the flesh." So with one fell swoop he scooped up Jamie from his bed, and carried him off to another cell in the tower, and locked him behind a grated door.

Then he went to Rob, and shook him till he woke.

"Get up, you lazy boy! Fetch wood and water, so that I may cook more food for your brother, and make him fat and juicy for my supper!"

Tears came to Rob's eyes, but the man grabbed him by the throat, and so he was forced to do as Bloody Sam commanded.

While he was in the forest fetching wood, he looked up and saw the crow perched above him.

"Why do you watch me so, crow?"

"I am the eyes of Bloody Sam," said the crow. "He sees you now through me. Sees, but cannot hear."

"He is a powerful magician," said Rob.

"Not so powerful as my old master, who he stole his magic from," said the crow.

"You talk as if you are a prisoner too!" said Rob.

"I am."

"You must help me, crow, lest my brother and I perish!"

"I will do so," agreed the crow. "Listen now, for I have a plan."

So they talked for a while, and then Rob returned to the tower, carrying as much wood as he could hold in his arms. Bloody Sam was waiting for him.

"Come, lazy boy, and set your load down! Then you must fetch another!"

Rob did as he commanded. Then he turned to the man and spoke.

"I have heard it said the younger the child, the sweeter the flesh," Rob told the old man, these, the crow had said, were Sam's own words. "That is why you plan to eat my brother, while I am to be your slave."

"That is true," said Bloody Sam.

"Then let me bring you a child still younger, to take my brother's place. Will that not be an even better meal?"

"It would," said the man, his greedy eyes already seeing a fat and juicy infant roasting above the fire. "But the younger ones are hard to find, and harder still to catch."

"On a farm not far from here there is a babe, a girl not more than a year old," Rob said. "If I bring her to you, will you let my brother and myself free?"

"I will," he said.

"Then I will go after I bring more wood," said Rob.

"Go now!" said Bloody Sam, practically tasting the child's sweet flesh.

"Alas," said Rob, and he could see the crow's plan was working, for Bloody Sam's hunger had consumed his common sense. "There is a fierce dog that guards her."

"A dog? Then you must kill it."

"With what?" said Rob. "I have no weapon."

"With this." And then Bloody Sam reached into his cloak, and pulled out from within it the bone of a chicken. "A poisoned bone, which the dog has only to chew on for a moment to perish."

"But this dog does not favor bones," said Rob.

"Then this," said Bloody Sam, reaching again into his cloak, and pulling out a small flask filled with a blood-red liquor. "One drop in the dog's water will be enough."

"But this dog drinks only from the mountain stream by the farm," said Rob.

"Then cold steel!" And now Bloody Sam reached within his cloak, and pulled out a golden key.

"This key unlocks my treasure room, in the basement of my tower. There you will find your pick of weapons."

And since this was what Rob had hoped for, he nodded and did as Sam told him. In the basement he found the treasure room, and unlocked it with the key. Inside were gold and silver and jewels piled high, and a store of weapons from those Sam had killed. Rob selected the finest sword, a blade almost too heavy for him to carry but one he felt sure he could wield when the time came.

And lying in the middle of all this treasure was a great book, which the crow had told him to look for. This was the book of spells by which the crow was held prisoner.

Rob turned the pages until he found what he was seeking, and read the words there. Then he took the sword, and brought Bloody Sam back his key.

"A fine weapon," said he. "Now go! For I grow hungry, and if you are not back by sunset, I will eat your brother!"

Rob took a sack from the kitchen then, to carry the infant in, and set off into the forest. But the sword hung heavy in his grasp, and his progress was slow. The sun was already past its highest point in the sky when he came upon the crow at the spot in the woods they had arranged to meet. Its eyes were closed, so Bloody Sam could not see where it was, nor what was about to happen.

"Did you find the book?" the crow asked.

"I did."

"And the spell within?"

"Yes."

"Hurry then!" said the crow.

Rob set down his sword and the sack. He drew in the dirt the shape of a pentagram, and stood within it, as the crow had bade him. Then he closed his eyes, and spoke the words he had seen written in the spellbook.

Spirit moved against the sun
And trapped within false form
By these words was spirit bound
By these words now reborn.

And when Rob opened his eyes again, before him he saw not a crow, but a great and noble owl, whose feathers were tinged with age, and whose voice was laced with majesty.

"Adonay, Lazay, Delamay, blessed be. I am myself again," said the owl. "Now we must hurry!"

So saying the owl took the sack in his beak, and Rob picked up the great sword in both his hands, and they ran through the forest as fast as they could.

The sun was setting as they drew near the tower, where they halted for a moment while Rob held the sack open, and the owl climbed within.

Then Rob knocked upon the tower door.

"Who is it?" came Sam's voice.

"It is I, Robert Rowland, returned with your dinner."

Sam cackled with glee then, and threw the door open.

"Come boy, bring it by the fire," said he.

And he did, and Bloody Sam took the spit from the fire, and beckoned him to open the sack so that he could stab the infant and roast it for his dinner.

But when Rob opened the sack, the owl flew out and startled Bloody Sam. And while his back was turned, Rob picked up his sword and chopped off the ugly old man's head!

Then the owl led him to the room where his brother, Jamie, was trapped, and Rob unlocked it with the golden key. Within, Jamie lay sleeping still. And at this sight, Rob smiled for the first time in days.

"Wake up lazy bones!" he yelled, and his brother yawned and stretched and opened his eyes. "For we are going home again!"

They took Bloody Sam's treasure back to their parents, save for the book of spells, which the owl claimed for its own. And there was food aplenty for all, and they all lived happily ever after.

**Inbox**

From:    witchfinder@netfree.org
To:      lomaxfellow@coolmail.com
Subject: Fairytale
Date:    Tuesday, Septmeber 14, 1999 12:08:09

Hah!
Do I have a story for you.

The Book of Shadows, by a writer named August Simpson. It's from one of
those old pulp magazines, Tales of the Uncanny, and may be pretty hard to
get hold of. Worth finding, though, especially if you're a Bloody Sam fan.

Unlike the fairytale, it has a twisted, unhappy ending.

Just the kind I like.

**From:**    **lomaxfellow@coolmail.com**
To:          witchfinder@netfree.org
**Subject:Re: Fairytales**
Date:        Tuesday, Septmeber 14, 2000 2:12:15

Jeff:

You're a sick puppy.

DECEMBER 13, 1999     $1.27 U.S.   $1.64 CANADA

WORLD NEWS

# BEAT BLAIR WITCH STRIKES AGAIN

**Shocking Maryland murders linked to two-hundred-year-old curse**

## NEWS EXCLUSIVE

## WORLD'S FIRST TALKING DOG

**"You stay!" Mutt Tells Master**

# Blair Witch Wacko Warned Tour Group

**by Betty Brant** / *World News Beat*

She saw death coming

Burkittsville, Maryland—Mary Brown, who got her fifteen minutes of fame when she appeared in the hit movie <u>The Blair Witch Project</u> last summer, warned the ill-fated Blair Witch Hunt tour group that they were headed for trouble.

According to Brown, she was the last person to see the five people in the group before they left for the Black Hills.

"I told him what was going to happen," Brown said. "But he wouldn't listen."

Brown, a notorious recluse, refused to reveal exactly who "he" was, or what she said. The BEAT has since learned that she and tour group guide Jeff Patterson were previously acquainted, so it seems likely that it was Patterson who she spoke with at the Black Hills Market outside Burkittsville on the afternoon of June 23.

Two days later, Erica Geerson and Tristen Ryler, members of Patterson's tour group, were brutally murdered. The three survivors stand accused of the killings.

---

# 70s Frozen Dessert May Hold Key to Eternal Life

Baby boomers, do you recall the 1970s frozen dessert called Whip'n'Chill? Well, if any among you were smart enough to save a box or two, you just may have a head start on the fountain of youth, according to Dr. Lazlo Bonricht of the Eastern European Scientists Union. "In my laboratory, we have been feeding the rats exclusively this Whip'n'Chill for the past three years. Tests show their skin and internal organs have maintained an unusual degree of plasticity," says Dr. Bonricht. The rats prefer Swiss chocolate flavor, the doctor notes, but will eat the banana as well.

---

# Wacky New Condoms Put the Surprise Back into Sex!

A new line of condoms developed by German pharmaceutical giant Harrison/Votel/Hochstetter borrows from an ancient Chinese custom to rekindle the passion in your love life!

"We call them fortune condoms," says Dr. Dedrick D. Piazza, executive director of the Hamburg-based consortium. "Each condom is fabricated and sealed within a plastic wrapper along with a piece of paper, which contains a sexual scenario to be played out by the lovemaking participants."

The condoms have been test-marketed to great success in Norwegian fishing villages, adds Dr. Piazza. "We expect to be on sale in North America within the year."

---

# Hollywood Go Home!

Town Residents Want to Be Alone

Hordes of tourists have inundated the small town of Burkittsville, Maryland, since the runaway success of this summer's blockbuster film <u>The Blair Witch Project</u>. The recent shocking series of deaths has brought the town even more notoriety—and the locals have had enough!

"You can't walk ten feet without getting a microphone stuck in your face or having a flashbulb go off," complained longtime resident Wanda O'Neill. "And anything that isn't nailed down, they steal for souvenirs!"

Others take a more pragmatic approach, like ninety-six-year-old Burt Atkins, who owns a store in town. "Can't say I dislike having the business," Atkins said. "But I agree people that come visiting should have a little more respect for those who live here."

Most of those locals, however, don't want respect. They simply want to be left in peace.

"We want them big-city types out of here," said Wilbur Whateley, a farmer whose cornfield was damaged when a tour bus took a wrong turn off a country road and plowed up half an acre of his land. "There ain't nothin' in them hills that's their business, anyhow."

# WITCH WAS KILLER!

**By Donald Mills** / *Exclusive to the Beat*

**Burkittsville Maryland**—In a bizarre new twist to an already bizarre case, accused killer Kim Diamond has told law enforcement officials that the real culprit behind the crimes she stands accused of is a two-hundred-year-old witch!

"I didn't hurt anyone," Diamond told a hastily assembled news conference. With lawyer Bart Amesby at her side, the self-professed psychic insisted that despite evidence to the contrary, she was not involved in any of the killings dubbed "The Burkittsville Murders" by the media.

The first of those killings took place on the night of September 20, when the bodies of five people—three tourists and their two local tour guides—were found, disemboweled, at the unfortunately named Coffin Rock.

Diamond was also with a tour group that night: the Blair Witch

## Goth Girl says: "We brought her back with us."

Hunt, run by her co-defendant in the murders, Jeff Patterson. Also in Diamond and Patterson's group were co-defendant Stephen Parker, and murder victims Erica Geerson and Tristen Ryler.

"That night in the woods was when all the trouble started," Diamond told reporters. "I felt a presence all around us."

Diamond nam that presence as t Blair Witch, a local le end, based on the sto of an actual perso which has received great deal of med attention since last su mer's hit movie, T Blair Witch Project.

The story of t Blair Witch dates back 1787, when a town call Blair stood on the la where Burkittsville is today. A wom named Elly Kedward was broug before the authorities and accused witchcraft. She was tried, convicte and banished. Since that time, beli ers say, Kedward has returned eve sixty years to claim vengeance on t town. They claim the witch has be involved in more than a dozen myste

# THE

us deaths during the last two
enturies. According to Diamond,
Edward was behind the recent
illings as well.

"Somehow Elly came out of the
woods with us," Diamond said.
She's the one who killed all those
eople."

Burkittsville Sheriff Ron
Cravens dismisses Diamond's
laims as nonsense. "She's been
eeding us this line since day one.
t's not supported by a shred of evi-
lence."

As an example, Cravens points
o the murder of convenience store
lerk Peggy Shuler, for which
Diamond also stands accused and
was captured on the store's security
ameras.

"What's on those tapes is not
hat really happened," Diamond
old the press.

# Killer Tour Guide Was Already Psycho

The man now accused of masterminding
the Blair Witch murders previously spent
four years in the looney bin—locked up on
his own mother's say-so!

Burkittsville Sheriff Ron Cravens
revealed to a stunned crowd of news
reporters that Burkittsville native Jeff
Patterson was institutionalized in 1992 after
kidnapping a neighbor's infant daughter
and fleeing with her into the Black
Hills forest.

"The doctors said he wasn't well
enough to stand trial," said a visibly angry
Cravens. "I'd like to know what made them
think he was well enough to release into
society. I'm sure the parents of the murdered girls would like to know that, too."

Patterson, who was 17 at the time of
the kidnapping, spent four years at the
prestigious Shelter Glen institution in New

Sussex, Massachusetts.
Reached for com-
ment, directors of the
institution declined
to make a public
statement. Patterson's
mother, Kathleen, has
also refused to speak to
the press since her son's alleged crimes.

The kidnapping took place on May
14, 1992. In a crime eerily reminiscent of
the infamous 1941 child murders committed by serial killer Rustin Parr, Patterson
stole 11-month-old Susan Walker from her
crib and set off into the woods with her.
Then-Deputy Ronald Cravens was among
the officers who captured Patterson and
rescued the infant girl.

No motive for the crime was ever
released to the public.

## Clark, Margaret

**From:**      dastern@mac.com
**Sent:**      Tuesday, February 10, 2000 17:11:16
**To:**        mclark@simonsays.com
**Subject:**   Supermarket Tabloids...

...take you to the most interesting places.

More on Patterson's institutionalization, from the local newspaper archives.

*Established 1846*

# FREDERICK POST

28 Pages   35 Cents

Frederick, Maryland

Friday, May 15, 1992

Volume 147, Number 137

# INFANT RETURNED UNHARMED: LOCAL YOUTH INVOLVED IN KIDNAPPING

by John Spencer
Staff Reporter

Burkittsville—An eleven-month-old Burkittsville infant, whose disappearance late last evening had sparked an intensive, countywide search by officials, was returned unharmed to her parents front doorstep early this morning.

Little Susan Marie Walker, the daughter of Chip and Frances Walker of 13 Primrose Lane, had last been seen by her parents sleeping peacefully in her room on Tuesday evening. When her mother came in to check on the baby, sometime near 10 p.m., she found the window open, and the child missing. Local and state law enforcement officials immediately launched a search for the infant, which was still ongoing this morning when Susan Marie was returned unharmed.

Authorities have a suspect in custody, identified only as a local youth who knew the Walker family. They would not release a name, because the accused is under eighteen years old. No motive for the kidnapping was cited.

# WALKER BABY'S KIDNAPPER IS SON OF FAMOUS LOCAL ARTIST

by John Spencer
Staff Reporter

Burkittsville—Authorities have identified the suspect in last week's kidnapping of a Burkittsville infant. He was named as Jeffrey Patterson, 17, the son of Kathy Sharrar Patterson of Braddock's Landing and Charles Patterson, a renowned local painter.

Jeff Patterson was intimately familiar with the Walker home, having served as a baby-sitter for the Walkers' two teenage sons on several occasions over the last year.

"We're shocked and saddened at Jeff's involvement in this crime," said Chip Walker, the father of the kidnapped infant. "We don't understand why he would want to put us all through this horrible experience."

Patterson remains in police custody at this time: authorities are still debating whether or not to charge him as an adult for his crime.

His mother has refused to comment to the press, and Patterson himself has supplied no explanation for his actions.

FREDERICK POST
Established 1846
Volume 147, Number 140
Frederick, Maryland
Monday, May 18, 1992
28 Pages
35 Cents

# PATTERSON NOT FIT TO STAND TRIAL

by John Spencer
Staff Reporter

Burkittsville—In a surprising development, a county psychiatrist has declared kidnapping suspect Jeff Patterson unfit to stand trial for his crimes.

Citing confidentiality issues, Daniel Lombard, the Frederick County social worker who examined Patterson, refused to give details on the substance of his report. However, sources within the Burkittsville Sheriff's office pointed to language in the report citing Patterson as an immediate danger to himself and others.

Lombard, a Mississippi native, has worked for the county health services department for ten years. His work was cited as exemplary by a number of colleagues.

Despite his credentials, prosecuting attorney Louis Chimes immediately denounced the decision, as did the parents of the kidnapping victim, eleven-month-old Susan Marie Walker, and family friends.

"This goes to show you that money can buy anything, even justice," said John Muller, one of the Walkers' neighbors. "Kathy waves around her checkbook, and folks around here line up to do what she tells them."

Patterson's mother, Kathy Sharrar Patterson, is estimated to have a personal fortune in excess of three million dollars, gained through the sale of her husband's artwork.

Through a spokesman, Mrs. Patterson announced that she would seek long-term care for her son at an unnamed, out-of-state facility.

Daniel Lombard

FREDERICK POST
Established 1846
Volume 147, Number 162
Frederick, Maryland
Tuesday, June 9, 1992
28 Pages
35 Cents

SHELTER GLEN

*"Time, and a Place to Heal"*

# Shelter Glen

34 Dunham Place • New Sussex MA 06783
William Von Seeley, M.D., Director

June 26, 1992

Kathleen Sharrar Patterson
Box 412 Rural Route D
Braddock Heights MD

Dear Mrs. Patterson:

On behalf of the staff here, allow me to welcome you and Jeff as members of the Shelter Glen Community. I spent a few hours with Jeff yesterday, and want to assure you that despite a few initial difficulties adjusting, he now seems to have made the transition to his new home.

We all recognize how difficult the decision was to hospitalize your son: nonetheless, I urge you to think of this as a step in a positive direction. Mental illness is a disease, one we learn about more with every passing day, one that is often as treatable as any other kind of disease.

Over the next few weeks, our staff will be evaluating Jeff's condition, and suggesting treatment protocols. Our goal, of course, is to return him to you as a full and productive member of society.

I urge you to contact me at any time with questions regarding Jeff's treatment or care during his stay here.

Sincerely,

Dr. William Von Seeley
Director

bp/WV

# Shelter Glen

SHELTER GLEN
PATIENT RECORD

**PATIENT'S NAME:** Jeff Patterson

**DATE:** June 29, 1992

**TYPE OF SESSION:** Initial Examination

**EXAMINING PHYSICIAN:** Hillary Seaver

**COMMENTS:**
Absence of disorganized speech
No mania, no flat or inappropriate affect
Delusion is fixed and specific but not grandiose
No cognitive impairments
Oriented x3
Intelligence average/above-average
Persistent auditory hallucinations
Delusions are of a persecutory/religious nature
ANXIETY IS HIGH!!!

**DIAGNOSIS:**
Schizophrenia,
paranoid type/rule out

**PROTOCOL:**
Haldol, 2 mg p.o.
Individual and group therapy

SHELTER GLEN
INTERNAL MEMORANDUM

TO: Administration

FROM: William Von Seeley

DATE: August 17, 1992

RE: JEFFREY PATTERSON

At the family's request, all sessions with this patient
are to be recorded and transcribed.

# Shelter Glen

SHELTER GLEN
PATIENT RECORD

PATIENT'S NAME: Jeff Patterson

DATE: September 13, 1992

TYPE OF SESSION: Individual Therapy

PSYCHIATRIST/CLINICIAN: Dr. Clayton Larsen

*How are you liking things here, Jeff?*
It's okay.
*Erica and Rachel seem to like you a lot.*
They're okay.
*But you didn't have a good time in group therapy.*
I wasn't aware I was supposed to have a good time.
*You didn't participate.*
I didn't know I was being graded.
*All right: Do you mind if we start talking a little about what happened—
the reason why you're here?*
I kidnapped the Walker's baby.
*That's right. Can we talk about why you did that?*
The younger the child the sweeter the flesh.
*I don't understand that.*
How long am I going to be here?
*Your mother thinks it's a good idea for you to be here right now. I can't
honestly say how long that's going to be.*
Right.
*So you've been taking your medicine a couple months now. How do you feel?*
About the same, I guess. Not really different. Why? Am I supposed to feel
different?
*Jeff. We're going to be spending a lot of time together, you and I, and
it's going to be very unpleasant if you turn everything into an argument.*
Sorry.
*Let's start over then.*
Okay. Hey: that picture—that's your boat?
*That's right. And my wife and kids. We went to the Cape last summer.*
We used to go down to Rehoboth Beach, me and my parents.
*You're an only child, is that right?*
Uh-huh.
*I've spoken with your mother before, but I obviously know very little
about your father. I have seen some of his paintings—*
Could we not talk about my father right now?
*All right. What would you like to talk about?*
This place. Shelter Glen. It's huge.
*There are a lot of people here.*
How many patients?
*Right now—about a hundred and twenty.*
And how many staff?
*All together? About forty.*
Forty people. To put humpty-dumpty Patterson back together again.
*Jeff...*
No, no. I don't mean that sarcastically. That's a good thing. I'd like
to be better. I'd like not to think about the things I think about.

May 19, 1993

Dear Jeff,

I just got off the phone with Dr. Larsen, who said
that you and he are getting along very well. I'm
glad to hear it. I'd love to hear all about it from
you – just a short note would be fine.

I know you're still angry at me, and I can
understand that. Believe me, I want you here at
home as much as you want to be here. It's just
not the right time for that now.

Dr. Larsen says that you are all planning on a trip
to Boston next weekend, to old "Ironsides". If you
like, I could come up and we could spend some
time together. You can call or write, or just let
Dr. Larsen know.

All my love

Mother

# Shelter Glen

SHELTER GLEN
PATIENT RECORD

**PATIENT'S NAME:** Jeff Patterson

**DATE:** September 8, 1993

**TYPE OF SESSION:** Individual Therapy

**PSYCHIATRIST/CLINICIAN:** Dr. Clayton Larsen

Hello, Jeff.
Hey, Dr. Larsen.
You seem to be in a good mood.
Yeah, it's a nice day.
I saw you through the window before—playing with Richie's dog.
Yeah, that's a nice dog.
You had a dog when you were growing up, didn't you?
Uh-huh.
Jeff, you seem a little disoriented today. Did you take your medication?
Uh-huh.
And you feel all right?
Pretty good.
Why don't we talk a little about your dog?
Rusty.
Yes, Rusty.
I saved him.
I know.
How do you—oh. My mom gave you the report.
I asked her for it, after she and I talked. This is quite a piece of work, Jeff. You were how old when you did it?
I don't remember.
First grade, let's see. You were probably six.
I guess.
So what made you write this?
It's what happened.
And this is Rusty?
Yeah.
And who is this, Jeff? On the rock, with you? [unintelligible]
Jeff?
I don't want to talk about it.

**CONFIDENTIAL**
For Internal Use Only

SHELTER GLEN
INTERNAL MEMORANDUM

TO: FILE

FROM: DR. CLAYTON LARSEN

DATE: March 12, 1994

SUBJECT: JEFF PATTERSON

Patient maintains a surface level of cooperation, but has consistently refused all attempts to discuss circumstances surrounding his delusions. I fear those delusions remain very much fixed in his mind.

Recommend an increase to 3 mg Haldol.

# Shelter Glen

SHELTER GLEN
PATIENT RECORD

PATIENT'S NAME: Jeff Patterson

DATE: August 5, 1994

TYPE OF SESSION: Individual Therapy

PSYCHIATRIST/CLINICIAN: Dr. Clayton Larsen

*Let's talk some more about the Blair Witch. Looking at my notes, I see
we left off with the hermit.*
Rustin Parr.
*Which brings us to 1969, and the Blair Witch Cult.*
Yeah.
*What's so funny?*
Cult. It wasn't really a cult: it was just a bunch of hippies, taking
drugs out in the forest, waiting for something spooky to happen.
*Why the name?*
I think it came from this old book they used to use in their cere-
monies. Or maybe the press made it up, I don't know.
*You said they expected something spooky to happen? Why do you think
they thought that?*
You know, where they were. The Black Hills. Lots of weird things
happened there.
*Jeff, have you ever heard the term "mass hysteria"?*
Sure. It's when people behave like lemmings. One jumps into the sea,
and everybody else follows.
*Exactly. I look at all these cases we've been talking about, of the
Blair Witch who haunts the Black Hills forest, and I see multiple
examples of mass hysteria. The children disappear, it's the fault of
the dead witch. A child drowns in a shallow river, it's the witch. An
old hermit goes crazy, and it's the witch. Everybody grew up listening
to stories of the Blair Witch, and now what you have in that part of
Maryland is a common thread of belief, waiting to be exploited.*
Okay. But there was no hysteria with the Cult. Nothing happened.
*But that belief is still there. I expect that if something were to
happen now, people would still jump up and down and scream "Blair
Witch! Blair Witch!"*
I guess.
*Do you see what I'm trying to get at?*
I didn't see the witch.
*What did you see?*
*Jeff?*
I don't know.
*People hear stories about the witch, they see the witch. You hear sto-
ries about Bloody Sam—*
She gave you those, too?
*Easy, Jeff. We're all only trying to help.*

# Shelter Glen

SHELTER GLEN
PATIENT RECORD

PATIENT'S NAME: Jeff Patterson

DATE: October 26, 1994

TYPE OF SESSION: Individual Therapy

PSYCHIATRIST/CLINICIAN: Dr. Clayton Larsen

*Hello, Jeff.*
We're taping again?
*We always tape, you know that. It helps me review our progress.*
Okay.
*Jeff? Erica told me about last night.*
Yeah.
*She said you had a nightmare.*
There was blood on the rock.
*What does that mean?*
What do you think it means? There was blood on the rock. That's not so hard to understand, is it?
*Easy, Jeff. Do you want something to drink?*
I'd like a fucking beer, is what I'd like, but there's no beer here is there?
*You don't need to shout. Would you like a glass of water?*
Okay.
*This dream, you said there was blood on the rock. Was this Coffin Rock?*
Maybe. Yeah, I guess.
*Whose blood was it?*
I don't know.
*Was it your father's blood, Jeff?*
No.
*You sound sure about that.*
It might be the baby's blood.
*The Walker baby?*
Yeah. It was supposed to be a trade. That's what I was supposed to do. For the magic to work. The way it did with Rusty.
*You brought the baby to Coffin Rock?*
Yes. But I didn't give him the blood. So it's all my fault.
*I don't understand.*
The blood on the rock now—that's my fault!
*Jeff?*
It was supposed to be a trade.

# Shelter Glen

Dear Mom,

I think it's time for me to come home. I don't think it makes any difference if I'm here or if I'm there. If I'm there, at least I can talk without watching every word I say.

You could come up and get me this weekend, and I'd be home for Thanksgiving. Do you think Jill's family would want to come to the house for dinner, like we did a couple years ago? I think that would help me, to be around friends and familiar surroundings again. I really do.

And if people are concerned, you know the police have those electronic monitoring bracelets now, where they can make sure you don't leave your house. I could wear one of those.

You don't have to call, you can just show up, whenever is good for you. Thanks, Mom. I love you.

Jeff

Shelter Glen

Dear Mom,

They won't let me say fuck you, but fuck you! for showing them my letter.

I guess they'll see this one too.

Don't bother coming up for Christmas.

Jeff

# Shelter Glen

34 Dunham Place • New Sussex MA 06783
William Von Seeley, M.D., Director

Kathleen Sharrar Patterson
123 R.R. 12 RFD 41
Braddock Heights MD

January 3, 1995

Dear Mrs. Patterson:

I appreciate your concern over the course of Jeff's treatment, and wanted to share with you our thinking at this point.

First of all, we as an institution and psychiatrists in general believe in the efficacy of drug therapy for illnesses like Jeff's. Given the recent high level of agitation Jeff has shown, both Dr. Larsen and our chief Dr. Seaver are recommending we switch Jeff from Haldol to another drug, Mellaril. We fully expect this will prevent further incidents like last October's.

We would also like you to consider the use of electroshock treatments for Jeff: for some people, this conjures up unfortunate images that have no resemblance to the true nature of this technique. I've taken the liberty of passing along a booklet which lays out the facts.

I understand from your secretary that you'll be out of the country until next week: we'd obviously like to address these issues as soon as possible, so call me at your earliest convenience.

Sincerely,

Dr. William Von Seeley
Director

bp/WV

**SHELTER GLEN**
**INTERNAL MEMORANDUM**

**TO: ALL CONCERNED**

**FROM: THE DIRECTOR'S OFFICE**

**DATE: January 13, 1995**

**SUBJECT: JEFF PATTERSON**

The patient's guardian has agreed to electroshock therapy.

Please set up a schedule to begin these treatments immediately, and provide me with a copy.

# Shelter Glen

*We haven't done this in a while.*
It feels like old home week to me.
*That's right—your mother was up yesterday.*
Yeah. She's doing good.
*And who was that girl who came with her?*
Jill. She was kind of my girlfriend in high school.
*Kind of?*
Well...I was pretty much of a geek. Spent a lot of time by myself, up in my room.
*Jeff. How old were you when the accident happened?*
Almost ten.
*Can we talk about it?*
Okay.
*It was just the two of you.*
We were way out in the woods by the time we made camp.
*That's why it was so hard to find you the next day.*
That's right. It was dusk. Just as the sun was going down. He was washing the dishes
we'd used for dinner in the stream, and laying them out on this big flat rock.
*Was this Coffin Rock, where you and your father were?*
No, no. We were all the way on the other side of the forest.
*Did you maybe think it was Coffin Rock? You meaning the nine-year-old you?*
Well... I suppose I could have thought that. I can't remember.
*All right. Go on.*
Well, I thought I heard something, out in the forest. Like a bear, or something
big, coming toward us. My dad said he'd check it out, just to ease my mind. So he
jumped up on the rock to get a better vantage point. And—
*Go on, Jeff.*
Yeah, that's when it happened.
*When what happened?*
When he slipped, and fell. I jumped up on the rock, and tried to help him but—
*You were only nine years old.*
There was nothing I could do.
*Of course not. You sat with him, though, that whole night. That was very brave.*
Uh-huh. I guess.
*Jeff? He slipped and fell. Are you telling me what you think I want to hear, or
what you really thought you saw?*
That's what happened.
*Jeff, I have Dr. Hoffmann's letters.*
Well, I know now that I was imagining things. I was hysterical, right?
*Of course you were. But it's important to understand why.*
It was getting dark, there were shadows everywhere, and all sorts of animals run-
ning around and flying by—
*And you were with your dad. In the woods.*
Yeah.
*Are you all right?*
Let me get a glass of water.

**Shelter Glen**

Dear Mom,

Sorry I missed your call, but I have a new job, at a place called Longview Digital. They do a lot of audio/video production, and post-production stuff. I'm just a gopher, obviously, but once in a while they let me play with the machines.

It was so good to see you again. Tell Jill I understand completely, okay? This place freaks me out a little bit, too, and I've had three years to get used to it. Tell her I'll call her when I get home, for sure. Which I think is going to be soon, I can tell by the way Dr. Larsen talks to me, and the way everybody else looks at me.

I can't wait.

Jeff

## Shelter Glen

*September 18, 1995*

*Mr. and Mrs. Chip Walker*
*13 Primrose Lane*
*Burkittsville MD*


*Dear Mr. and Mrs. Walker,*

*I guess I'm about the last person in the world you'd ever expect to get a letter from. I know you probably never want to think about me again, or hear from me, but I just wanted to write and say that I was sorry for what I did. I hope you can forgive me.*

*I guess the only explanation I can offer is that I went a little bit crazy. Up here at Shelter Glen, they've been giving me treatments and I understand now that everything I was thinking was all just part of one big delusion. I don't know if that makes it any easier for you.*

*I just want you to know that I am very sorry for what happened, and thankful that Susan is all right.*

*I hope you're all doing well.*

*Sincerely,*

*Jeff Patterson*

**TO: ALL STAFF**

**FROM: THE DIRECTOR'S OFFICE**

**DATE: October 11, 1995**

**RE: JEFF PATTERSON**

As many of you are aware, this is Jeff Patterson's last week here. While we will all miss Jeff, this is obviously an occasion worth celebrating.

Please join us Friday evening at 7:00 in the Kraepelin Room for cake and a chance to bid him farewell.

*Good Luck!*

# Shelter Glen

SHELTER GLEN
PATIENT RECORD

PATIENT'S NAME: Jeff Patterson

DATE: October 12, 1995

TYPE OF SESSION: Individual Therapy

PSYCHIATRIST/CLINICIAN: Dr. Clayton Larsen

How was the party?

It was great.

I'm so sorry I couldn't be there.

That's all right: I knew I'd get to see you again today.

So how does it feel to be going home?

Great. So great I can't even begin to tell you. So what are we supposed to do here?

Well, I just thought we could—

You want me to tell you how crazy I was?

No, that's not necessary.

I was crazy though, to take the Walkers' kid. Thinking I could strike a deal with the devil.

Very poetic.

Yeah. It's from one of the Ian Connors stories.

I thought I recognized the phrase.

You've read some of those?

I've read all of them.

Wow.

Don't look so surprised, Jeff. They were important for me to read, to understand what you were thinking. We put the one—The Book of Shadows—in your file.

That's funny.

Why?

I was thinking about writing a screenplay based on that one.

Really? I didn't know you wanted to be a writer.

I don't know what I want to do, truthfully. I have to finish high school first. Then...I don't know. I'm pretty lucky. We've got the money so that I can take some time off, maybe do some traveling.

Work on your screenplay.

Exactly.

I think that's a great idea. Horror movies are bound to make a comeback.

Yeah, I think so.

So who would you get to star in it?

Well, my dream cast.... I guess for Sir Ian, I would get Peter Cushing, you know from the Hammer films?

Sure.

Except he's dead.

It's a dream cast. And the American? His sidekick.

John Davis. That's easy: Bruce Willis.

Peter Cushing and Bruce Willis: that would be quite a combination.

Yeah, wouldn't it.

And Bloody Sam?

I don't know... that's a tough one.

Some things are better left to the imagination.

Right.

So this is goodbye, Jeff.

Yeah. Unless I run into the Blair Witch when I get home.

Jeff—

I'm kidding, I'm kidding. You don't have to worry about that. Believe me, I'm cured. Boy, am I ever cured.

Tales of the

# Uncanny

November    25¢

A Hawk O'Brien Story
by Wallace Biester

JOHN COLE YOUNGER
PAUL SCOTT SHANNON
K.T. RYAN

August Simpson's Terrifying
THE BOOK OF SHADOWS
*A full-length thriller*

A MAGAZINE OF THE WEIRD AND SUPERNATURAL

# *Tales of the Uncanny*

Registered in the U.S. Patent Office

| Volume 3 | CONTENTS FOR NOVEMBER 1939 | Number 6 |

Published bimonthly by Tales of the Uncanny, 42 Park Street, Baltimore, Maryland. Application for second-class entry pending at the post office at Baltimore, Maryland. Single copies, 25 cents. *Subscription rates:* One year in the United States, $1.50 for 6 issues; Canada, $2.75; elsewhere, $3.00. The publishers are not responsible for the loss of unsolicited manuscripts, although every care will be taken of such material while in their possession. The contents of this magazine are fully protected by copyright and must not be reproduced either wholly or in part without permission from the publishers.
HOLLAND WHITCOMB, Editor.

**TALES OF THE UNCANNY ISSUED**
**15th JANUARY, MARCH, MAY, JULY, SEPTEMBER, NOVEMBER**

*Sir Ian Connors and John Davis track an ancient evil across the Atlantic—and find themselves face-to-face with their own long-buried past! A full-length thriller from the author of "The Monkey's Other Paw."*

# THE BOOK OF SHADOWS
## by August Simpson

It was the damnedest thing I ever saw, and I was about to say so. But the widow Penrose beat me to it.

"Oh my heavens! Mr. Hawley!" she said. "The table!"

The Hawley Mrs. Penrose was referring to was our host—Mr. Alistair Hawley—and the table was the round wooden one in front of us, covered by a red cloth. Nothing much out of the ordinary about this table, no sir...unless you count the fact that it was floating up about an inch off the ground.

Besides the red cloth, there were also five linked pairs of hands on the table, belonging to myself, Miss Jennifer Smith (Mrs. Penrose's private secretary), Hawley, Mrs. Penrose, and my employer, Sir Ian Connors.

We were all participating in a séance, being conducted by Mr. Hawley in great style. His eyes were closed, he was moaning softly to himself, and like I said—

The table was floating in the air.

It had gone up slowly, barely an inch at first, starting with the side directly opposite Hawley. The wooden leg there trembled for a moment, as if afraid to launch itself off solid ground. Then, apparently having found the courage to give up on gravity, it rose a full three inches all at once.

"Oh, but this is impossible," whispered Miss Smith. Her deep blue eyes were wide with wonder, and I felt her hand squeeze mine tighter.

I guess I ought to introduce myself here. My name's John Davis. I'm an American, born and raised in Red Rock, New Mexico, but for most of my adult life—since the year I turned eighteen and realized there was a lot more to the world than the cattle drive—London's been my home. I came here seeking adventure and escape from the day-in, day-out sameness of the rancher's life, which I have to admit I've found in spades. Especially over the last ten years, working as I have for Sir Ian Connors.

Him, I'll get to in a minute.

"You have that which I asked you to bring, madame?" Hawley asked.

"Oh, yes. Something that belonged to my husband, yes," said Mrs. Penrose. "Miss Smith has his pocket watch. Jennifer?"

The young lady next to me reached into her purse, and came out with the watch, which hung on a long silver chain. She handed it to Hawley.

"Excellent." He held the watch in his hands a moment: the letter "L" was burnished into the silver faceplate, identifying it as a Leicester timepiece. It was probably worth more money than Hawley had earned in the last year. The way he caressed it, he was clearly aware of its value.

"Your husband treasured this piece, Madame?"

Mrs. Penrose nodded energetically. "He carried it with him everywhere."

"Then he will doubtless sense its presence across the ether." Hawley put the watch down in the middle of the table, and we all joined hands again.

"We wish to contact the spirit of Cornelius Penrose," began Mr. Hawley. "Mr. Penrose, are you there?"

Sir Ian and I exchanged a glance.

During his lifetime, Cornelius Penrose had been one of London's wealthiest industrialists. The fortune he left to his wife was valued by some in the tens of millions of pounds. Since Mr. Penrose's passing, the widow had run through a half-dozen financial advisers while trying to decide what to do with her husband's money.

Now she'd decided to ask Mr. Penrose directly. With the aid of Mr. Hawley, who Miss Smith quickly came to suspect of having designs not just on his fee, but a significant chunk of the Penrose estate. She had relayed those misgivings to Sir Ian and myself the previous week, when she came to see us at 21 Plymouth. Once on the case, Sir Ian and I discovered her suspicions were well founded. Prior to becoming a medium, Hawley had been a confidence man. His last job: a securities swindle that netted him a few hundred pounds and six months in jail.

Sir Ian and I felt the odds were good Hawley had come across our names while researching his new line of work, so we decided to use different ones. I had come to the séance as General Rod Honeycutt, a Texas cattleman, and Sir Ian was my manservant, Mr. Northall. Our excuse for being at the séance? A romantic interest on my part in Miss Smith, who I would gallantly permit no harm to come to.

"Mr. Penrose," Hawley repeated. "Are you there?"

The table lifted off the floor once more, then settled.

"By the veil of Ashtoreth," Hawley began. "In the name of Asmodeus—"

"You fool," Sir Ian said clearly. "Stop this at once."

Hawley looked up as if he'd been slapped.

"I beg your pardon?"

"You are trifling with powers beyond your ken," Sir Ian said.

"Your ken being the local second-story men," I added.

"Gentlemen?" Hawley's gaze went from one of us to the other. "What is this nonsense?"

"The nonsense is this charade," said Sir Ian, standing. "Which I am putting a halt to at once."

"Really, General Honeycutt," said Mrs. Penrose, leaning across the table to speak to me in hushed tones, "can't you do something about your man?"

"His name is not Honeycutt, madame," said Sir Ian. "And I am not his man."

"What—who are you two?" asked Mrs. Penrose, her eyes darting back and forth from one of us to the other.

"We are your servants in this matter, Madame, engaged by Miss Smith." He stood now, and stared down from his new

vantage point at Hawley. "This man is John Davis. And I am Sir Ian Connors."

"Connors!" gasped Hawley. He jumped to his feet and started backing away from the table. "What chicanery is this?"

"Chicanery in a good cause, sir," said Sir Ian. "While your chicanery serves only your own greed!"

Sir Ian nodded to me then, a prearranged signal at which I moved behind Hawley and pinned his arms behind his back.

"What is the meaning of this outrage?" Hawley sputtered. "Unhand me at once!"

"Hold him, Davis!" Sir Ian stepped back from the table and advanced on the two of us. "I will show you the meaning of outrage, sir."

Hawley shrank back in my grasp as Sir Ian approached. Then, in one swift motion, Connors drew open the long coat Hawley was wearing.

"There, Mrs. Penrose," said Sir Ian. "There is your miracle of levitation revealed!"

The widow gasped, as did Miss Smith, for affixed to Hawley's belt, pointing upward toward the ceiling, was a large metal hook!

"I will show you, Madame, how the spirits levitated this table." Before Hawley could move, Sir Ian had the belt off the scoundrel and fastened around his own waist. He took Hawley's seat at the table.

"Observe." He took Hawley's chair at the table. "I seat myself so that the hook points upward and catches the lip of the table—so. Then"—he put his hands on top of the table—"I lean back and apply downward pressure with my hands at the same time and—voila!"

Before our eyes, the table rose again— a full half foot off the ground.

"Oh!" Mrs. Penrose's hand went to her breast. "I never! Shame on you, Mr. Hawley. To take advantage of my good nature thus. You will be hearing from my solicitors, I can assure you of that!"

Hawley went limp in my grasp, and hung his head. I felt sorry for him—for a moment.

"Incredible," said Miss Smith. She gazed adoringly on Sir Ian. "Your reputation does not do you justice, sir. I only wish there was something I could do to properly demonstrate my appreciation."

I smothered a grin. A lot of young ladies had tried to show their appreciation to Sir Ian during the decade I'd worked for him: he allowed none of them to penetrate his armor. Sir Ian's passion was his work: exposing crooks like Alistair Hawley, and more importantly, preventing them from actually arousing the spirits they called on.

"These mediums, these so-called psychics," Sir Ian had once told me, "they are like children, given a colorful box of matches to play with. Our duty, Mr. Davis, is to prevent them from accidentally starting a fire."

It was a lesson Sir Ian had learned through bitter, firsthand experience. I refer you to the case of The Monkey's Other Paw, and the fate of Victoria Summers, the young woman who had once been Sir Ian's fiancée. Her body lay now in an immaculate, luxuriously appointed suite in the private wing of London's Bethlehem Hospital.

Her mind, unfortunately, was elsewhere.

The horrific circumstances were the direct result of a single mistake on Sir Ian's part, a miscalculation that colored his every waking moment.

I took back the belt from Sir Ian, and used it to bind Hawley's arms. Meanwhile, Sir Ian was politely declining the attentions of the lovely Miss Smith.

"I thank you for your kind offer, my dear, but we shall have to discuss it at length another time. I must send for the police now, and then Mr. Davis and I are to return home, where we are immediately to begin work on another case."

Again, I had to smother a grin. I suspected this "other case" Sir Ian spoke of was just a ploy to avoid Miss Smith's attentions. My guess was that we had nothing ahead of us at home but an evening of cigars and brandy.

After surrendering Hawley to the local constabulary, Sir Ian and I took a horse and buggy—excuse me, a trap, as they call them here—back to the house at 21 Plymouth. We found an unexpected visitor waiting for us.

Mr. Brian Lobell, editor of the *London Budget*, and a frequent guest at Sir Ian's dinner table, had been admitted by Pendrake and sat now in the office, hands clenched in his lap.

"Sir Ian," said he, rising from his chair. "I hope you will forgive my intrusion at this late hour."

"I trust the matter is urgent." Sir Ian crossed behind his massive desk and sat. "Davis and I have just finished running a most cunning scoundrel to ground, and I had hoped to spend the remainder of my evening with a cigar and a good book."

Lobell nodded. "It is, Sir Ian."

"Then sit. Tell me what is troubling you."

"It is not a 'what,' sir, but rather a 'who.' One of my best reporters, who has taken it on himself to suddenly disappear and—"

"I wondered what had become of Mr. Stackpole," said Sir Ian. "Do go on."

Lobell's jaw dropped. "It is Stackpole. But—how did you know?"

"His byline has not appeared in your paper these last two weeks. Nor have I seen him at the Windsor Club tennis courts, which he and I both frequent. It seemed a fair assumption."

Lobell nodded. "When you put it that way, of course."

Of course. I smiled. A lot of Sir Ian's deductions seemed obvious with the benefit of hindsight. The trick was to take that leap in logic without the benefit of signposts.

Sir Ian frowned. "Do you seek help finding your man, sir? If so, surely the police, or a private detective bureau would be more likely candidates to assist in your search."

Lobell sighed. "I'm making a muddle of this, aren't I? Perhaps I had better start over."

"Let's have something to clear your head first." Sir Ian rang the bell on his desk, and Pendrake appeared in the doorway. "The '98 Clavendell, Mr. Pendrake. For myself and Mr. Lobell."

"Make it three," I said, which earned me a haughty glare from Pendrake, who—even after ten years—regarded me as an intruder in the house. He bowed to Sir Ian and disappeared down the hall, returning a few moments later with a tray bearing three snifters and the Clavendell. He poured us each a glass. Mine came up a bit short, and I gave him a dirty look as he exited the room.

"Ah," said Lobell, taking a sip and rolling it around in his mouth. "Remarkable. Just the thing I needed. Thank you, Sir Ian."

Sir Ian nodded. "Of course. There are few troubles in life that a good brandy cannot help ease. And now, Mr. Lobell, you must tell me Stackpole's story—from the beginning."

"Very well," said Lobell. He settled back in his chair, arranged the brandy on the table at his elbow, and began.

"Stackpole is my best correspondent. He knows it, and I know it. So I grant him unprecedented latitude. Unprecedented." Lobell shook his head, as if he couldn't quite believe how free a rein he'd given the man. "Well, he came up with this idea of going up to Lancaster for the three-hundredth anniversary of the witch trials. To use that as the foundation of a series of pieces on witchcraft. Bloody Sam, and all that."

"Who?" I asked.

Lobell grinned. "'Black of heart, forever damned. Beware the grasp of Bloody Sam.'"

"A figure of superstition in the western counties." Sir Ian clipped the end off a Coronado, stuck it in his mouth, and

began puffing. Unlike brandy, the Cubans were not something he shared around with his guests—or even me. "I would enjoy reading those pieces."

"As would all of us," said Lobell indignantly. "But now—I fear he's gone stark raving mad!" The man reached into his shirt pocket and pulled out a telegram. "Look at this wire!"

The irritated look on Sir Ian's face changed as he read through the wire, replaced by an expression I rarely saw him exhibit.

Surprise, bordering on shock.

"Good Lord," he said, letting the wire dangle from his hand.

I snatched it away from him, and read it through myself.

I reproduce it now for the reader's benefit.

7 August 1912

LOBELL:
SORRY NOT BEING IN TOUCH STOP. PIECE ON BLOODY SAM WITCHES TAKEN DETOUR STOP. SAILED EVENING AMERICA STOP.
RETURN WITH STORY CRUSH STANDARD AND TIMES STOP. REFER TO GRIMOIRE CALLED THE BOOK OF SHADOWS STOP.
WILL WRITE STOP.
STACKPOLE

"The nerve of the man," Lobell said. "Nothing from him for two weeks, and then this! And the wire is two days old—he's sailed already! Boarded a ship from Liverpool bound for Baltimore."

"What is this Book of Shadows Stackpole refers to?" I asked.

"Well, that's why I'm here!" Lobell exploded. "I have no bloody idea! Sir Ian?"

We both turned to my employer...who sat stock-still at his desk, not having moved a muscle since I took the wire from his hand.

"I had thought it a fiction," he whispered. "Like the unexpurgated Clavicula Salmonicus, or the Mad Arab's Necronomicon. But if it is real..."

"Sir Ian? Are you all right?" I asked.

He shook his head as if to clear it. "Forgive me, gentlemen. It is just a shock to see that particular volume named...in a telegram, of all things."

"Then you know what it is?" Lobell leaned forward.

"I do." My employer stood then, and walked to the west wall of the office, which was lined floor to ceiling with bookshelves. Those shelves contained an impressive collection of rare books, manuscripts, and privately printed volumes Sir Ian had traveled the world over to obtain.

He pulled one book—no thicker than a pamphlet, really—off his shelf, and began flipping through it. "This is Chattelier's treatise on white magic, and—here we are." His finger traced a line of text down the page. "'Rituals of the Coven'—this describes the ceremonies performed by these witches." He cleared his throat. "'The Priestess reads from a book of ancient writings, said to be called 'The Book of Shadows.'"

"Their prayer book, it sounds like," I said.

"It is akin to a prayer book." Sir Ian closed the volume in his hand, and put it back in its place on the shelf. "Though it contains not just rituals, but beliefs, incantations, spells, and all manner of healing lore. Each coven is charged with keeping its own Book of Shadows."

"This is something they use every day?" Lobell frowned. "Where's the story in that?"

Sir Ian shook his head. "You miss the point, sir. The name "Book of Shadows" is now given to the book each coven uses, but it originally derives from a single, mythic source. A book that belonged to the greatest practitioner of magic the world has ever known." He raised his gaze to mine. "Merlin, the Enchanter."

I raised an eyebrow. "Merlin...as in King Arthur's Merlin? As in Knights of the Round Table Merlin?"

"Exactly. The Book of Shadows was Merlin's grimoire. His spellbook. The most powerful text in the history of the occult. It disappeared from the sight of man more than a thousand years ago."

"And now, Stackpole thinks he's found it."

Sir Ian turned to Lobell suddenly. "You must ask him to wire me with details."

Lobell nodded. "Of course. Only..." A gleam came to his eye. "Something occurs to me, Sir Ian, hearing you talk about this Book of Shadows. Perhaps this is a bigger story than I originally thought."

"It most certainly is." Sir Ian sat back down at his desk then, and picked up his cigar from the blue and gold ashtray (a gift from the Grand Vizier of Bashirrad). "It could be akin to the discovery of Excalibur. Stackpole is entirely right to say this piece would propel you far ahead of all your competitors."

"Well, then. I have a proposition for

you." Lobell smiled. "How would you like to go to America after him?"

Sir Ian inhaled deeply on his cigar, and nodded at Mr. Lobell to continue. "What do you have in mind?"

"Stackpole's a good reporter, but he's wandering far off his turf with this piece. Politics, foreign affairs, those are his areas of expertise. I'm not sure our readers will buy this piece on the supernatural from him at all."

"So my job?"

"Find him. Talk to him. Evaluate what he's found out: you're the authority in this field. Make sure he's not writing something that will make the *Budget* look like a pack of fools. Perhaps you can write something of your own to go with his pieces."

"Mmmm." Sir Ian leaned back in his chair, and gazed upward. On the ceiling of the office was a mural of the zodiac and all its associated mythological figures. Sir Ian studied that mural in silence a moment, puffing on his cigar. A cloud of smoke wandered across the ceiling, settling in front of the Twins.

Pendrake came in and freshened Sir Ian's drink, then Lobell's, pointedly ignoring my attempts to catch his eye.

Lobell asked. "Are you interested?"

Sir Ian puffed again. "Mr. Davis will have to accompany me."

"Of course." Lobell smiled. "I'll prepare a draft on the paper's funds to get you started."

"Then we are agreed," Sir Ian said.

"Except for the crass details," I said. "Money, and all that."

"Money?" Lobell named a figure.

I smiled, and doubled it.

He frowned, we bargained, and eventually met in the middle.

"I'll leave you gentlemen to pack, then." Lobell drained the last of his brandy, and stood. "You'll wire me with developments?"

"Of course," I said. "Do you have any ideas on how we might begin our search for Mr. Stackpole? America's mighty big."

"Ah. I almost forgot. I have another wire here," said Lobell, again rummaging around in his pockets, "a confirming wire, from the inn he'll be staying at in America. Here." He pulled out a piece of paper, and handed it to Sir Ian. "I'll book you two rooms there as well."

"That will be fine," said Sir Ian. "We'll find passage on the first ship available."

We shook hands all around. Then Pendrake appeared again and showed Mr. Lobell to the door.

"I'm a little surprised," I told Sir Ian once we were alone. "Knowing how you feel about America."

Sir Ian rang for Pendrake again. "Overridden in this case by the possibility of finding this book. The odds of its existence are slim, of course, but...ah, Mr. Pendrake. Davis and I will be leaving on the first ship tomorrow for America. You'll please pack my trunk for an extended journey: though I shall require only two suits. The blue, I think, and the grey wool: it will be fall, will it not, Davis?"

"It will," I said. "But Baltimore, as I recall, is hot and humid well into the season. You'd be better off leaving the wool behind."

Sir Ian shook his head.

"It is not Baltimore we go to, Davis, but a more remote part of Maryland." He looked at the piece of paper Lobell had left. "A town called Burkittsville."

A fierce storm greeted us in the middle of the Atlantic, delaying our progress, so that it was mid-September by the time we finally reached Maryland, and a day after that when we at last laid our bags down by the front desk of the Burkittsville Inn.

"Can I help you folks?" asked the clerk.

"I expect you can," I said. "I believe you have a couple of rooms set aside for us. John Davis, Sir Ian Connors."

"You bet," the clerk said, turning the register around to face us. "Sign right here, and I'll get you your keys."

"Thanks," I said.

"Sir, huh?" asked the clerk, looking over Sir Ian as he handed us our keys. "You'd be English then, that right?"

"Correct," said Sir Ian.

"We got another English fellow visiting out here. Name of Stackpole."

"Hugh Stackpole," I said. "We know him."

"He's an odd one," said the clerk.

"Is he in?" asked Sir Ian.

"He's in all right," the clerk said. "Don't know that he's up to visitors, though."

"Why?" I asked. "What's the matter with him?"

The clerk shook his head. "Not for me to say."

Just then the door behind us swung open, carrying with it a hint of lilacs. A woman's perfume. The kind Victoria Summers, Sir Ian's unfortunate fiancée, had favored.

Just behind the perfume, Victoria Summers herself entered the room.

"Excuse me, gentlemen," she said, striding past Sir Ian and myself, who stared after her like a pair of slack-jawed schoolboys. "Hello, Albert. Do you have any mail for Mr. Stackpole?"

"Nothing, ma'am. But these folks here are looking for him."

"Indeed?" she asked, turning back to us. "And you are?"

I kept telling myself it couldn't be her, that she lay, for all intents and purposes, dead to the world, an ocean away.

Sir Ian found his voice first.

"Sir Ian Connors," he said. "This is Mr. John Davis. We are friends of his from London. And you are?"

"Miss Claire Cooper. I live just down the road, in Jericho Mills."

"Remarkable," said Sir Ian, taking her hand.

She looked at him curiously. "I beg your pardon."

"Remarkable. You look uncannily like someone I once knew."

"A friend of yours, I hope?"

"Oh yes," said Sir Ian, smiling.

She smiled back.

Of course she wasn't Victoria: for one thing, her voice was entirely different. No accent. As was her posture: Victoria had been bred to be a lady at the finest finishing schools on the Continent; Miss Cooper was an American through and through. Still, her deep blue eyes, upturned nose, and above all her hair—

a long, thick, flowing red avalanche of curls—were virtual duplicates of Victoria's. They could have been twins.

"I hope you are Mr. Stackpole's friends as well," Miss Cooper said. "Because he could certainly use some at this moment."

"Why? Is something the matter with Mr. Stackpole?" I asked.

"Dr. Madison has been treating him for nervous exhaustion, as well as injuries he suffered a few days ago," Miss Cooper said.

"Nothing too serious, I hope?"

"No, no. He spent the night camping in the forest nearby, and was attacked by something." She glanced over at the clerk then, and lowered her voice. "He has been suffering from hallucinations as well."

"Hallucinations?" Sir Ian asked. "Of what sort?"

Miss Cooper leaned closer. "He claims," she said, still whispering, "to have seen our local bogeyman—or bogey-woman, in this case." Her gaze locked on Sir Ian's. "Our Blair Witch."

Sir Ian prevailed on Miss Cooper to join us for an early supper in the inn's dining room.

"Three days ago," she told us, "I was riding into town for some supplies, when I found Mr. Stackpole lying in the road, half-conscious, bleeding from a wound at the back of his head."

"Given him by this witch?" Sir Ian picked up his knife and fork and started cutting at a piece of the fried chicken Miss Cooper had insisted on ordering for all of us.

"He cannot say for sure: his back was turned."

"But he did see this witch?"

"So he claims." Miss Cooper stifled a grin as Sir Ian struggled with his food.

"Is something the matter?" he asked, seeing the amused look on both our faces.

"It's easier if you use your hands," I told him. I picked up a leg of the chicken, and took a big bite. "See?"

"Is this permitted?" Sir Ian looked to Miss Cooper, who nodded encouragingly. Then he set down his silverware, picked up a wing off his plate, and bit into it.

"Delicious," he said. "Please, Miss Cooper—continue with your story."

"There's not much more to tell. Mr. Stackpole has been in his bed since the incident, recovering."

"I'd like to hear more about this Blair Witch," I put in.

She nodded. "It is a local legend, going back well over a century, when a town called Blair stood in the very place where Burkittsville is today."

"Stood? What happened to it?"

"Abandoned in the late 1700s, after all the town's children mysteriously disappeared. Stolen away by Elly Kedward, the witch. According to the legend, the witch reappears here every sixty years to take her revenge on the town's children." She set down her chicken, and wiped her hands. "The last incident occurred some twenty-five years ago."

The waiter came over then, and freshened our drinks.

"Thank you, Ben," she said. "The

chicken is delicious. My compliments to Anne."

"She'll be pleased to hear that, Miss."

"My compliments as well," Sir Ian said to the waiter. But his gaze remained fastened on Miss Cooper's (admittedly lovely) face.

"You were saying—about the last incident with this witch?" I prompted.

"Yes. I believe it was 1887, when this took place. A little girl vanished, and a search party of five men went after her. The girl was found a few days later, but the men..." She shook her head. "They never came back. They were found a few days later. Butchered, their bodies arranged in the shape of a pentagram."

Sir Ian, in the middle of taking a sip of wine, choked and started coughing.

The fit lasted a good ten or fifteen seconds.

"Excuse me," he said finally.

"Are you all right?" I asked.

"Yes, just surprised." He wiped his lips with a napkin. "Arranged in the shape of a pentagram, you said?"

"Yes, that's right."

"Good Lord," Sir Ian said. "It's Bloody Sam, all over again."

"Bloody who?" Miss Cooper asked.

"That's just what I said," I told her.

"Bloody Sam. A figure of legend, in England. Bloody because he sold his soul to the devil in exchange for the lives of five innocent men. Whose bodies he butchered, and then arranged in a pentagram."

I whistled in amazement. "That's quite a coincidence."

"Does this have to do with Mr. Stackpole's story?" Miss Cooper asked.

"Very likely," Sir Ian said.

"Are you reporters as well?" Miss Cooper asked.

Sir Ian and I exchanged a glance. We hadn't decided who we should be here in Burkittsville, whether our true occupations would be a help or a hindrance.

"We're freelancers—of a sort," I replied, deciding to skirt the issue. "Helping Mr. Stackpole on his story."

"About the Book of Shadows," Miss Cooper said.

Sir Ian nodded. "That's right."

"You'll be interested to know, then," she said, setting down her knife and fork on her plate. "He's found it."

"He's what?" I'd never seen Sir Ian looked so surprised twice in one evening: if he'd been drinking at that instant, I believe he would have choked again and gone into another coughing fit.

The waiter appeared again.

"Miss Cooper, gentlemen. We've got some lovely pumpkin pie this evening."

Sir Ian held up a hand. "A minute, sir. Miss Cooper, you say he's found the book?"

"Yes. That's what he told me." She smiled at the two of us. "You really must try the pie, Sir Ian. You don't know what you'll be missing."

"I will have pie later." He pushed back his chair from the table, and stood. "Please. Take me to Mr. Stackpole."

Stackpole's room was about as far away from the ones Sir Ian and I had as possible, on the second floor of the inn and down the hall.

"He may still be sleeping," Miss Cooper said as we came to a door marked with the number five. She knocked softly. "Mr. Stackpole?"

She waited a moment, then turned to us.

"We'll have to come back."

Sir Ian shook his head. "No. I must see that book."

"I don't know where it is."

"I will find it."

"You are a stubborn man, Mr. Connors." Miss Cooper offered a slight smile. "Very well. But we'll have to be quiet: the doctor is concerned he conserve his strength. He doesn't want the hallucinations to recur."

"Of course," Sir Ian said. "I understand."

She grasped the doorknob then, and slowly turned it. The door creaked as she pushed it open.

The room was dark within. Miss Cooper crossed quickly to the far wall, and turned on the gas lamp that hung there. A warm light suffused the room.

The inn's food had been simple but well made, and the room was no different. A small cherry wood dresser, a night table, and a sturdy-looking four-poster in the middle of the room, on which a tall, thin man lay sleeping.

"Mr. Stackpole, I presume?" I whispered to Sir Ian, who nodded affirmatively.

"He's lost weight."

"The poor man," Miss Cooper said, staring down at him fondly.

As if he knew we were talking about him, that poor man suddenly opened his eyes, and sat up with a start.

"Who—"

"Easy, Mr. Stackpole." Miss Cooper placed a hand on his shoulder and forced him gently back down in bed. "Some friends of yours are here."

Stackpole swallowed, and nodded. Then he looked around the room.

"Sir Ian," he whispered. "Is that you?"

"Stackpole." Sir Ian laid his hand over Stackpole's. "Lobell sent me—he was worried about you."

"Worried about his story, more likely," said Stackpole. His eyes met mine over Sir Ian's shoulder. "You must be John Davis."

"I am," I said. "How are you feeling, Mr. Stackpole?"

"Better than a few days ago, I daresay." He lifted his head off the pillow and touched the back of it. "Ow."

"What happened?" I asked. "Who hit you?"

"I—" he shook his head. "I'm afraid I don't remember very clearly: it all happened so quickly."

"It was a very hard blow." Miss Cooper turned to us. "The doctor thinks it may have affected his memory of the incident."

"I suppose so." Stackpole grimaced again, and rubbed his temples. "But I believe it was the witch. I said so before, didn't I, Miss Cooper?"

"You did." She looked disturbed. "Gentlemen, we really must let Mr. Stackpole rest."

"The Book of Shadows," Sir Ian said, ignoring her. "Miss Cooper tells me you have found it."

Stackpole nodded. "I have."

Sir Ian's eyes blazed with excitement. "It is here, now—in your room?"

"No, I'm afraid not. That is what I was searching for, in the woods. When I was attacked."

"But you know where it is?"

"I believe I do, yes."

"Incredible." Sir Ian shook his head in disbelief, and smiled. "You are on the verge of a discovery that beggars the mind, Mr. Stackpole. Tell me quickly"—he turned and glanced back at Miss Cooper, as if to say he understood her desire to let Stackpole rest— "how you traced the book here."

Stackpole nodded. "In the remains of a tower, in Pendle Forest, I found a fragment of paper, a sheet torn from a book."

"I should like to see this fragment," Sir Ian said.

"That, I have with me now." Stackpole raised his arm and pointed to a black leather satchel that lay next to the dresser. "In there."

Sir Ian had already crossed the room and was opening the satchel.

"The Shakespeare folio: the fragment lies flat within that," Stackpole continued.

Sir Ian pulled out the folio, a large, oversized volume closer to the size of a newspaper than a normal book, and laid it down on top of the dresser. He began flipping through pages. I stood close by, peering over his shoulder.

"Here it is," he said softly.

A yellowing sheet of paper, no bigger than a piece of stationery, lay neatly tucked between two pages. It was torn along one long edge, and covered from top to bottom with faded black writing.

"That's not English," I said.

"No." Sir Ian lowered his head and studied the page intently. "Old Welsh, I believe. I would date it at the ninth century; perhaps earlier." He moved his lips silently for a moment, sounding out some of the writing before him. "*Llyfr O Cisgodion,*" he said, pronouncing it like "Efear o Sisgodeon." He turned back toward me excitedly. "Book of Shadows."

Gooseflesh raised on my arms.

"You must tell me more." Sir Ian returned to Stackpole's bedside. "Where you first found this, who gave it to you, how you determined what it was."

"Of course." Stackpole turned to Miss Cooper. "If I might trouble you for a cool glass of water, and a cloth for my head."

"I'll bring you those things," Miss Cooper said. "But then we all need to leave. Sir Ian, Davis?"

"Madame," said Sir Ian. "You do not understand. What we have here—"

"What we have here, will be here in the morning," Miss Cooper said firmly. "Mr. Stackpole, you do recall Dr. Madison telling you that you needed your rest?"

"I'm not an old woman, Miss Cooper."

"No, of course not. But you do want to live to be an old man, don't you?"

He sighed. "Perhaps it would be better to rest. Sir Ian, can you wait till morning?"

"If I must," he said. "May I take the fragment to my room, to examine it further?"

"Of course," said Stackpole.

Sir Ian carefully closed the Shakespeare folio, and tucked it under his arm.

"We will speak tomorrow," he said. "After I have deciphered this."

Miss Cooper brought Mr. Stackpole his

drink and a cool cloth. Then we all said good-night, and left the room.

"Thank you, gentlemen. We do not want his hallucinations to return." Miss Cooper smiled. "Some of that pie now, perhaps? And then, if you'll permit me, I'll show you the sights of our little town."

"Sounds good to me," I said.

"You go on, Davis," said Sir Ian. "I want to look this over—" he held up the folio, and the manuscript page therein—"at once."

I noticed a flash of disappointment cross Miss Cooper's face as Sir Ian turned on his heel and started down the hall.

"Don't take it personally," I told her. "There's not a woman alive that can compete with a dusty old book, as far as Sir Ian is concerned."

She glared at me.

"You're very forward with your assumptions, Davis. Which I do not welcome." She spun on her heel, and started downstairs. "You're welcome to join me for pie, or not."

Stifling a grin, I followed.

The pie was good, and Miss Cooper proved a charming guide to the town's historic sights, which included a house where President Abraham Lincoln (a personal hero of mine) had once spent the evening. Still, the tour turned out to be briefer than I would have expected (I suspect Sir Ian's absence probably had something to do with that), so that it was only eight o'clock when we parted ways for the night, and I returned to the inn.

There was a light coming from under the door of Sir Ian's room, directly across the hall from mine. He would be up until all hours, no doubt, examining the fragment Stackpole had given him. I thought about checking in on his progress, then decided to wait until morning. Breakfast, the clerk had told us, was served at seven: we would talk then. I read for a while in my bed (Conan Doyle's "The Hound of the Baskervilles") and fell asleep sometime around nine-thirty.

At midnight, I awoke suddenly, the sound of a bloodcurdling scream echoing in my ears. For a moment, I thought I had imagined it: the howl of the ghostly hound chasing after Hugh Baskerville, as in the story I had just finished.

Then the howl came again. And I realized it was the scream of a man, not a beast.

It sounded, in fact, like Mr. Stackpole.

I was out of bed and slipping on my clothes when an urgent knock came at my door. I opened it to find Sir Ian standing there, holding a candle.

"Did you hear that?" he asked.

"I did. Stackpole?"

He nodded. We took off at a trot. A door opened as we ran past, and a man I hadn't seen before peered out.

"What's all the ruckus? Decent folk are tryin' to sleep here!"

We ignored him, and continued down the hall to Stackpole's room.

The door was wide open. He was nowhere in sight.

Sir Ian and I looked at each other.

"Where do you suppose—"

The scream came again, now from outside.

Taking the stairs two at a time, we burst through the doors of the inn.

Fortune was with us: the moon shone

bright and the night sky was clear, so we had light to see where we were going. And to see, down the road the inn stood on, a tall, thin figure, running as if for its life, disappear over a rise.

Sir Ian snuffed out the candle, threw it to the ground, and we gave chase.

"What on earth is he running from?" I asked between breaths.

Sir Ian, a step ahead of me, turned.

"His own imagination, I fear."

I nodded grimly. Miss Cooper had been right to worry for his health: Stackpole's hallucinations had apparently returned.

We cleared the rise, and stopped for a moment to get our bearings. Ahead of us the road curved to our left, and entered the woods.

We saw Stackpole veer to his right, and set off across a field bordering the road.

"For a sick man," I said, still trying to catch my breath, "he's got a very healthy set of lungs."

"We can cut him off. There," Sir Ian said, pointing ahead of us to a small hill. "Come."

And he set off in pursuit again. I followed, a step behind, at a pace that felt even faster than our previous efforts.

Stackpole was no more than twenty yards ahead of us when we cleared the field.

"Leave me alone!" he cried, turning back. "You don't understand! She'll get you, too!"

He started up the rise Sir Ian had pointed out before: now that we were closer, I could see a wooden fence running the entire width of the hill, just before the top of it. Not a very sturdy fence, though:

Stackpole literally ran through it as he crested the rise.

A second later, we heard him scream again.

Sir Ian and I reached the fence, and saw that Stackpole had simply stepped over a portion of it that had fallen. We jumped over it ourselves, and quickly came to the top of the rise.

I was still a step behind Sir Ian, which probably saved my life. His eyes were better than mine.

"Davis!" Sir Ian cried. He put out his hand, halting my progress.

Two feet before us, the hill abruptly ended.

Beyond was nothing but the horizon.

"It's been blasted away." Sir Ian pointed down and ahead of us: I could see some kind of machinery gathered below. "It's a mining operation of some kind."

"Help!"

We turned then, and saw Stackpole.

Ten feet away from us, he hung over the edge of the cliff, holding on for dear life with one hand, the other windmilling frantically beneath him.

"Hold on!" I shouted.

We made our way carefully down the hill till we reached his side: Sir Ian was there first.

"Easy," Sir Ian said as he reached Stackpole, and grasped hold of the man's one hand with his two. "I've got you."

Stackpole shook his head, wild-eyed. "Do you see her?"

"There's no one here but us," I assured him. I circled behind Sir Ian and came around Stackpole's other side.

"Give me your other hand," I told him.

His eyes widened. I heard a noise behind us, and turned.

I thought I saw something dart over the rise then, just out of my field of vision.

Stackpole screamed again.

He slipped out of Sir Ian's grasp, and fell.

It took us a good half an hour to make our way safely to the bottom.

We found no trace of his body.

As the sun rose, we found ourselves back in the inn's dining room, drinking coffee, and trying to explain what had happened to the local law enforcement authorities. Those local authorities being a stout, barrel-chested man named Carl Bracher, the town sheriff, and his deputy, an older fellow who he simply called Prickett. Bracher was not happy about being up so early, and seemed determined we should all share his misery. He woke the innkeeper and had him brew up a pot of coffee, he had Prickett take a team of dogs up to the mine and search for Stackpole's body, and he had Sir Ian and I answering the same series of questions over and over for close to an hour.

"I wanna make sure I understand you fellows," Bracher was saying. "You and Mr. Stackpole work for the same paper?"

Sir Ian sighed. "Constable—"

"Sheriff."

"Sheriff, we've been through this already."

"Like I said—I wanna make sure we're on the same page."

"I assure you, in regards to the death of Mr. Stackpole, everything happened exactly as Mr. Davis and I have told you."

"Then where's the body?"

"I'm sure I don't know."

"What do you think happened to it?"

"I think if you search again in full daylight, you'll find it," Sir Ian said.

"I had the dogs back there for an hour." This came from Prickett. "There ain't nobody in that mine, Carl."

"So what happened to the body?" Bracher asked again. He took a sip of his coffee. "You see my problem."

Prickett came and stood next to the sheriff. "Hey, Carl. Ain't this the fellow that they say saw the witch?"

"Yeah. So?"

Prickett shrugged, and looked at the ground. "Well, I just thought—"

"Oh, for God's sake." The sheriff shook his head. "Don't you start up with that."

"Well you ain't lived around here long as I have, Carl." Prickett shook his head. "There's a lot of strange things in those woods."

"There is no damn Blair Witch!" Bracher said.

"Sheriff, can we go to bed?" I asked.

He glared at us. "Go on. Just be around this afternoon. I may have some more questions for the two of you."

Sir Ian and I trudged slowly upstairs.

"I plan on sleeping until noon," I told him when we reached our respective doors. "Please observe the 'Do not disturb' sign."

"I want to show you something first, Davis." Sir Ian opened his door, and held it for me. "Come with me, if you would."

Sir Ian's room was identical to mine, as mine was to Stackpole's, the only difference being that Sir Ian had set his trunk down in the middle of the floor, and was now using it as a makeshift table. The fragment Stackpole had given him lay spread across that table now.

"There is something puzzling about the fragment Mr. Stackpole gave me."

"It's fake?"

"No, not so far as I can tell with the equipment at my disposal here. What is puzzling is this," he said, pointing to the ragged edge of the document.

"What? The tear?"

"Precisely." He motioned me closer.

"What do you notice about that portion of the page?"

I looked at it carefully.

"Nothing."

"Here. Look closer." He reached into his case, and handed me a magnifying glass.

"The ripped edge," I said. "Compared to the others, it's a lot whiter."

"Precisely," Sir Ian said. "The color is different."

"So what does that mean?"

"Books age from the outer edges in: the acids and moisture attack the edges first."

"So?"

"So, if this page had been ripped out of the book long ago, as Mr. Stackpole has implied, you would expect all the edges to have yellowed relatively evenly. Instead, we have this."

"So this page was torn out recently," I said.

"So it would seem."

I frowned. "I don't see how that could be."

"Neither do I." Sir Ian shook his head. "Regardless, the page itself seems genuine enough. Which makes our next task plain."

"Find the Book of Shadows. And we have to wire Lobell, and tell him what's happened."

"Of course." Sir Ian's expression grew reflective a moment. Then he turned to me. "May I share a confidence, Davis?"

"Sure."

"I have been thinking of Miss Summers. She has been in Bethlehem how long now?"

"Going on seven years, I believe."

"Yes," he said. "Seven years, that she has lain as if in a coma. Seven years, during which the finest doctors in all the world have been seeking a cure for her, to restore her sanity. And they are no closer today than they were the day we brought her there."

I nodded. I had a feeling he was trying, in a roundabout way, to bring up the subject of Miss Cooper with me.

But I was wrong.

"What I am thinking," he said, "is that we may now be on a verge of a cure ourselves."

I took a deep breath. I had known Sir Ian a decade now, and in all that time, I had only seen him lose control on one occasion: when he first discovered Victoria Summers, lying as one dead, in the third floor antiquities room at 21 Plymouth. Since that event, he had presented the same face to the world each day: composed, implacable, unflappable. A face like a mask, one that held the raging turmoil of emotions inside him.

I didn't know if it was such a good idea to take that mask off.

"Sir Ian—"

"I shall not get my hopes too high," he said quickly, as if he was reading my mind. "But Merlin's grimoire! This book is rumored to contain magic the likes of which has not been seen since the world was young. Spells to transmute the elements, preserve life immortal, even to raise the dead. Why not to rejoin body and mind?"

"Why not?" I said. "There's the little matter of finding it, though. That's a mighty big forest out there."

"Of course," he said. "Although for the first time in years, I have hope. There is nothing wrong with hope, is there, Davis?"

"No sir," I said. "Of course not."

"Very well." he nodded. "Get some sleep. When morning comes, I will see both Lobell and Miss Cooper are made aware of this evening's unfortunate events. And then—" He closed the piece of paper within the folio. "Then we leave for the forest."

I slept until almost noon.

When I finally dressed and came downstairs, I found Sir Ian and Miss Cooper having lunch in the inn's dining room. After recovering from the shock of Mr. Stackpole's accident, she was now determined to accompany us on our expedition into the woods. She even had an idea as to where to begin the search.

"There is an old hut that some people swear once belonged to the witch," she told us. "I can take you there."

I ate quickly, and the three of us visited the General Store, where we outfitted ourselves in high style with Mr. Lobell's money. As I went to pay, the man behind the counter smiled at Miss Cooper.

"I like what you've done with your hair," he said.

Miss Cooper blushed for a moment, as if she'd been caught making up her face for an important date, then smiled. "Thank you, Bert."

We hired a carriage to take us some distance along the road out of town, where the trail Miss Cooper knew began.

"We should be able to get to the hut in about two hours," Miss Cooper said.

I glanced down at my watch—just past three o'clock—and then up at the sun.

We had, I guessed, some three hours of daylight left.

Sir Ian and I carried food and water in our bags, as well as the materials necessary to start a fire, should we become lost and have to spend the night in the forest. Luckily (I had enough of sleeping out under the open stars back in New Mexico to last me a lifetime) those supplies turned out not to be necessary.

It was with the last traces of light left to us that we came to a slight clearing in the woods. Before us, nestled so snugly in the branches of a huge elder tree that it was almost invisible, stood a small wooden building.

"There it is," said Miss Cooper. "Elly Kedward's hut."

I shook my head: the word I would use to describe the dwelling before us was ramshackle: it was crooked, uneven, and badly in need of repair.

"We're going to find the Book of Shadows in there?" I shook my head. "I find that difficult to believe."

"Stranger things have happened, Davis." Sir Ian set down his bag at the edge of the clearing, and stood silent a moment, studying the house, and its surroundings, listening to the noises of the forest.

"I sense something," he said finally.

I waited for him to elaborate, but instead he bent down, pulled some candles from his bag, and started toward the cabin. At the entrance to the shack, Sir Ian stopped in his tracks.

"There is writing here." He lit a candle, and held it near the doorframe. "Hieroglyphics of some sort. I don't recognize them."

"Let me see." Miss Cooper sounded strangely anxious. She leaned over Sir Ian's shoulder. "These weren't here before."

"Before?"

"I was out here a few summers ago," she said quickly. "How else would I know how to find the place?"

I nodded. "Of course," I said, frowning. Something felt wrong to me, suddenly, but I couldn't put my finger on exactly what.

Sir Ian opened the door, and entered the cabin.

The candle shed light on an interior as badly run down as the outside. There were holes in the wall, and roof, and the floorboards creaked and groaned with every step.

A chimney and crumbling fireplace stood along the cabin's far wall. Next to them on one side was a desk, with a book on it.

"Good Lord," said Sir Ian. He crossed the room in a flash and held the candle over the desk.

"This is it, Mr. Davis." He sat down and began flipping through the pages of the volume before him. "The Book of Shadows."

I didn't know what to say.

Just then, the cabin door opened again.

Hugh Stackpole stepped through, holding a pistol in one hand.

"Gentlemen." He smiled. "How wonderful to see you again."

Once again, Sir Ian was the first to find his voice.

"Mr. Stackpole. What do you mean by this?"

"By this?" Stackpole smiled, and held up the gun. "Why, it is for you and Davis. I mean to shoot you with it."

I shook my head. "Why?"

"Why?" The smile on his face twisted into something bitter, and ugly. "Do you remember a girl named Victoria Summers, perhaps?"

Behind me, I heard Sir Ian draw a sharp breath, and step forward.

"Of course I do," he said. "What is your relation to Miss Summers, sir?"

"My relation?" His eyes were pinpricks of fire, blazing in the dim light of the room. "I was as close to her as the pea to its podmate. I pushed her pram when she was a newborn, played at catch with her as a child, helped her with her numbers as a schoolgirl. I was her escort to the Plantaganet Ball, at her coming-out. I was ever the shoulder she sought out when trouble found her. My relation to Victoria Summers, you ask?" He set the sack carefully down on the floor, and took a step forward, leveling the gun at Sir Ian. "I was her brother, sir. And she was my beloved, only sister!"

"I never knew she had a family."

"She and my father fought," said Stackpole. "He didn't approve of her independent ways, so she left home, and changed her name. It took me two years to find her. But by then it was too late. She lay already in her bed at Bethlehem, no better than a vegetable! Thanks to your unfathomable arrogance, Sir Ian!"

My employer shrank back under Stackpole's verbal assault, but only a moment. "I cannot deny my guilt," he whispered. "But with this"—he turned back to the Book of Shadows—"I believe I can save her, rejoin mind and body. I believe—"

Stackpole laughed. "You have been guzzling your beloved brandy for far too long, Sir Ian! You actually believe this supernatural nonsense!"

"Hold on," I interrupted. "Whatever business you have with Sir Ian and I, you can at least let Miss Cooper go."

Stackpole smiled. "Have no worry on that count."

Miss Cooper detached herself from our group and walked to his side.

He put an arm around her waist. She smiled up at him.

"She and I will be leaving together."

I shook my head. "Now I really don't understand."

"I met Miss Cooper two years ago, in London," said Stackpole. "She is an actress."

"A very good one, wouldn't you say?" she asked. Her voice was entirely different now, as was her manner. And as I watched, she reached to the back of her head and twisted something in her hands. In a second, the long, flowing red curls that had made her look so much like Victoria Summers were lying in Miss Cooper's hand.

"A wig," Sir Ian said.

"Precisely. A distraction, you might say."

He smiled at her. "And there's another one for when she was Dr. Madison."

"So the witch's attack—"

"Faked as well, as was my deadly fall." He shrugged. "I had hoped to guide you into a more deadly fall of your own that evening, but it was not to be."

"Why go to all the trouble of killing us here?" Sir Ian asked. "Why not simply shoot us in England?"

"You underestimate your own worth, Sir Ian. Your death there would have drawn the attention of Scotland Yard's finest. Here, your passing falls under the provenance of Sheriff Bracher and his man Prickett." He shook his head. "It's a good thing I plan to lead them back here to your bodies, otherwise I suspect your disappearance would remain unsolved."

"And who do you plan to blame for this crime, Stackpole? Who will you say killed us?"

"Why, isn't it obvious?" he asked, and exchanged a smile with Miss Cooper. "You two are to be the latest victims of the infamous Blair Witch."

Miss Cooper dragged another chair in from the shack's other room, and while Stackpole held the gun on us, tied us back to back in the two chairs.

"How did you arrange for Lobell to send us here?" I asked.

"All I had to do was mention something vaguely related to the occult in my wire, and I knew he would go running to you to cover his bets," Stackpole said.

"Stackpole," Sir Ian pleaded. "Listen to me. This elaborate scheme for vengeance you have concocted, there is no need for it! Let us take the book with us, back to England. I will restore your sister—"

"With mumbo-jumbo, Connors? You will bring her out of a coma with mumbo-jumbo, like some Congolese witch doctor?" He shook his head. "I should like to see you, crouched over an iron kettle of noxious herbs, chanting to yourself on the polished linoleum floor of Bethlehem hospital. That would be a sight, indeed. One almost as pitiful as the cackling old women in Lancashire from whom I stole your priceless Book of Shadows."

Sir Ian shook his head. "My God, man, is there no end to your foolishness? You stole this book from a coven of witches?"

"And they were almost as upset about it as you. The one old woman cursed me, and said Bloody Sam would find me, no matter how long or far I ran." He smiled. "But it worked. It brought you running."

"Stackpole, you are an intelligent man, I know you are," said Sir Ian. "Listen to me, I beg you. There is a power that surrounds this simple dwelling, a power beyond human understanding. I have sensed it. Its purpose is evil. It seeks blood." Sir Ian fastened his gaze on Stackpole's. "Feed its desire, and you risk consequences unimaginable."

"If I don't feed it," Stackpole said, "I expect you'll keep talking. And that, I've had quite enough of."

"Hugh," Miss Cooper said uncertainly. "There was some strange writing carved on the door. Did you do that?"

"Claire, my dear. Please. Behave like the sensible woman I know that you are." He handed her the gun, and from his cloak, pulled a gleaming, razor-sharp knife. "I'll be through very shortly."

"May God have mercy on your soul," Sir Ian said.

"I'm not the one going to meet my maker, Sir Ian."

I heard the slash of a knife through the air, then and the sounds of cloth tearing.

I turned my head, and saw a crimson stain spreading on Sir Ian's white shirtsleeve.

"You have brought blood into this place," Sir Ian said. "Let whatever happens next be on your head."

As if on cue, a great wind suddenly shook the shack.

Stackpole's smile faltered.

"Hugh," said Miss Cooper. "I'm frightened."

"Stop behaving like a hysterical old washwoman," said Stackpole sharply. "Wait outside, if you have to."

I heard cloth tear again. Sir Ian grunted.

Miss Cooper walked to the cabin door.

"Sir Ian, I should have taken off your coat before I tied you up," Stackpole said. "It would have been so much easier to carve the skin."

"Untie me. I'll take off his coat for you," I offered.

"I can't open the door," said Miss Cooper. I turned and saw she her standing a few feet away from it, confusion etched on her features. "The knob won't turn."

"What?" Stackpole asked.

"The door." Her voice was little more than a whisper. "It won't open."

"Well it must have jammed. I'll be with you in a moment."

The wind came again, harder this time. It seemed to strike the house like a giant fist.

"Sir Ian?" I asked.

"Hugh, please!" Miss Cooper stood at the door, grabbing the handle with both hands. "Please! Come let me out!"

"Oh for God's sake, woman. Get a grip."

The wind struck again. A pane of glass in one of the cabin windows shattered.

Miss Cooper ran to the other side of the cabin, to the door in the next room. "It won't open either," she said.

With a sigh of exasperation, Stackpole set down the knife and turned toward her. "You're getting hysterical over nothing, Claire. I'll—"

He must have seen what I saw, at exactly the same time.

All around the entrance to the cabin, where the strange writing had been carved, the doorframe was glowing.

Miss Cooper screamed again, and now Stackpole himself shrank back toward the cabin wall.

"What in God's name..." his voice trailed off to nothing.

"It's coming," whispered Sir Ian.

The doorknob turned.

"Davis!" Sir Ian said, his voice amazingly calm. "Close your eyes! Look not on its face!"

The cabin door swung open.

I quickly closed my eyes, but not before I caught a glimpse of something filling the doorway. A huge, broad-shouldered figure.

In the light from the rising moon, steel gleamed.

Stackpole screamed, and a second later, Miss Cooper's full-throated cry of terror joined his.

The floor creaked, and now I heard the sound of footsteps, scrambling this way and then that across the cabin floor. Stackpole and Miss Cooper, trying to escape whatever it was that had entered the shack.

And then the floor shook, as first one booted foot, and then another, struck the ancient wooden boards.

No, I realized, listening closer. The sound I was hearing was not two boots striking the floor.

*It was more of a clip-clop, clip-clop, clip-clop: a man with a wooden leg, making his way across the room.*

"Don't look," whispered Sir Ian. "As you value your life, Davis, don't look!"

The wind howled again, louder than ever, so loud that I could no longer hear Miss Cooper or Stackpole scream, or even my own heartbeat. It was like a thing alive, moaning in agony under the cruel hand of whatever forces had commanded its appearance.

Then, above that unholy din, I heard Stackpole scream one final time: a scream of sheer terror, the scream of a man facing the end of existence itself, head-on.

That scream I shall never forget, until my dying day.

When I opened my eyes again, the cabin was still.

The ropes that had bound us were gone, dissolved away into thin air.

Sir Ian and I stood.

"The Book!" he shouted, racing for the desk.

It had vanished. As had Miss Cooper.

"Look," I said, pointing to the

half-open cabin door. Miss Cooper lay on the ground, neck twisted at an unnatural angle. Stackpole was next to her, on his back, half-in, half-out of the shack. His eyes were wide and unseeing, his shirt torn open.

Strange writing of some kind—the same as that which I had seen on the doorframe, which I saw now were there no longer—was carved into his chest. Blood still oozed from the cuts.

Drool trickled from the corner of his mouth.

"We'd better get him to a doctor," I said, kneeling over him.

Sir Ian shook his head. "Too late for that."

Sheriff Bracher was going to put us in jail and keep us there until we "satisfactorily explained" what had happened in the woods. Then a wire arrived from London, apparently in response to an earlier query he'd made. Whatever it said, he was suddenly a firm believer in the story Sir Ian and I had come up with on the way back from the cabin in the woods, that Stackpole, having clearly faked his own death previously, was also responsible for whatever fate had befallen Miss Cooper.

We spent another night at the inn, and the following morning we arranged for transport back to England.

In my room, I stood at the window a moment, and looked out toward the horizon. In the distance, the wooded forests where Miss Cooper had perished, and Hugh Stackpole had met, perhaps, a far worse fate, lay like a lush, blackish-green carpet across the gently rolling hills.

There was a knock at the door; Albert, the innkeeper, come to take my bags.

As he walked out, Sir Ian walked in.

"The coach is here."

I nodded, but found I was unable to turn away from the window just then. It was my imagination, of course, but in the shadows cast by the fading sunlight, the vast, carpeted forest seemed to actually be moving, like the tide washing in, growing closer, ever closer to the helpless, unaware town of Burkittsville.

Sir Ian came and stood by me.

"I look forward to being back in London," he said. "And the voyage home."

"Hopefully, Bloody Sam won't be returning on the same ship."

Sir Ian managed a faint smile. "I do not think that force we encountered in the woods—whatever it was—will soon leave here, Davis. This is an evil place, and evil is drawn to it." He turned away from the window. "Now more than ever, I fear greatly for the good people of Burkittsville."

We left the room then, and went downstairs to the waiting coach.

*Sir Ian Connors and John Davis return in "The Sorceress at Delphi," coming soon to the pages of Tales of the Uncanny.*

## Clark, Margaret

**From:** dastern@mac.com
**Sent:** Friday, February 18, 2000 21:12:16
**To:** mclark@simonsays.com
**Subject:** Bloody Sam and the Blair Witch

Who put these two together in Jeff Patterson's mind?

More on Charles Patterson from archives of the Frederick Post.

Father and Son

FREDERICK POST
Established 1846
Volume 131, Number 76
Frederick, Maryland
Monday, March 15, 1976

# Local Artist Takes Long and Winding Road to Success

### by Michael Fuhr

After years of struggling to make ends meet, painter Charles Patterson of Braddock Heights, age fifty-eight, has finally hit the big time. Over the weekend, his canvas "Woodland Autumn" sold to an unnamed buyer at New York City's Greene-Lavalier Gallery for $275,000.

"I think Charles's work will become increasingly in demand," said Arnold McClelland, spokesman for the gallery. "He's the first painter I have seen whose work fuses the classical forms with the colors and techniques of our new era."

Patterson, a thin, dark-haired man who still speaks with a trace of an English accent (his family moved to this area in 1932), began working as an artist right out of high school. In 1936, he made his first sale to a local pulp magazine, "Tales of the Uncanny," and was soon a regular contributor to many of the era's other pulps, such as "The Spider", "All-American Sports Stories," and "Other Worlds." His best-known work of this period was done for "Tales of the Uncanny," when he provided illustrations for a series of stories featuring the occult detective Sir Ian Connors.

Though writer August Simpson, a Baltimore native, created the series, it was Patterson who suggested incorporating bits and pieces of local mythology, in particular the ghost known as the Blair Witch, into a story called "The Book of Shadows." It remains a favorite memory for him.

"August loved the idea of bringing Connors to America. He came up here for the weekend, and we went camping in the woods to soak up the atmosphere."

After the war, when the pulp market dried up, Patterson moved to Baltimore himself and lived with Simpson, doing a little advertising work and, by his own admission, a lot of drinking.

In 1965, Simpson was killed in an accident. Patterson moved back to the Burkittsville area and started painting seriously again. He lived like a virtual hermit in the woods for a few years, coming down only to buy groceries and painting supplies. Patterson credits his growth as an artist to this period in time; certainly the themes he continues to work with today—nature as a physical, tangible presence, the mixture of the real and surreal within the same canvas—date to this period.

Another pivotal event occurred in the late sixties when Patterson met Kathleen Sharrar. Sharrar, formerly a singer with the pop group Hillary's Butterfly, had come to the area along with group leader Leroy Creegan for the 1968 Hagerstown Happening Rock Festival. When the festival ended, the group decided to stay.

"They were all living like a commune, in this run-down old factory up in Jericho Mills, not too far from where I was," Patterson recalls. The communal living situation was typical for the sixties, as were the religious rituals Patterson found the group performing.

The so-called Blair Witch Cult disbanded in 1970, after Leroy Creegan's mysterious disappearance. Patterson and Sharrar got married and moved to Braddock Heights. He kept painting, she found work as a schoolteacher, and last year, after two previous miscarriages, their son Jeff was born.

Just because he's finally got money, Charles Patterson doesn't expect his life to change very much. "I'm still going to be buying my groceries down at Culpepper's, my gas at the Shell Station, and my newspaper at W.W. Smith's," he says. "And for at least the next few years, I'm going to be changing a few diapers."

# HOW TO DO MAJIK

## BY JEFF

FIRST GRADE

MAJIK IS REL AND
YOU CAN DO IT.
I DID IT.

ONE TIME MY DOG RUSTY
GOT SICK. DAD SED
HE WAS GOING TO DIE.

SO I USED THE
MAJIK SPELL BOOK

AND RUSTY GOT
ALL BETTER!

THE END

*Established 1846*

# FREDERICK POST

Volume 139, Number 262     Frederick, Maryland     Monday, July 17, 1984

# Local Painter Injured in Tragic Accident

**Ron Weinstock**

Renowned local painter Charles Patterson was seriously injured late Saturday afternoon in an accident in the Black Hills forest. Patterson and his nine-year-old son, Jeffrey, were camping when the painter apparently slipped and fell on a large rock. He suffered massive head trauma.

The two were found by another couple hiking in the woods the following afternoon. Patterson was rushed by ambulance to Frederick County Hospital, where he is currently listed in stable condition. The extent of brain damage, as well as the prognosis for his recovery, cannot be ascertained at this time.

Nine-year-old Jeffrey was also hospitalized for shock relating to the incident: he was released early this morning into the custody of his mother, Kathleen Sharrar Patterson.

Dr. Emil Hoffmann
62 East 62nd Street Suite 1A
New York NY 10019


September 14, 1984


Kathleen Sharrar Patterson
Box 412 Rural Route D
Braddock Heights MD


Kathleen:

    After spending some time last week with Jeffrey, I believe I can safely allay your concerns regarding his condition. For all intents and purposes, your son has just gone through an experience equivalent to losing a parent: his desire to have you constantly in his sight is a natural reaction. Allow him these next few weeks to cling to you: he needs them.

    His nightmares and so-called hallucinations are also perfectly understandable. Put yourself in his position: your father lies seriously injured in your arms, night has fallen, and you are a little nine-year-old boy, alone in the forest. Young children make monsters out of the coat flung across the bedroom chair, or the hat hanging on a doorknob: Jeff had a whole wilderness full of strange sights and sounds to set his imagination loose on.

    Please understand me: I do not want to dissuade you from taking Jeff to see someone. I think it would help to have him talk all this out, to have someone who can draw everything out of his subconscious into the light, where he can see things for what they really are. That someone can either be you, or a professional: perhaps, ideally, both.

    Please do keep me posted on both his, and Charles's condition: you are all in my thoughts.


Sincerely,


Emil

# Unhappy Anniversary for Patterson Family

By Lelia Whickham-Kelly

Tomorrow morning, Kathleen Patterson, as she has done for each of the past four years, will drive down U.S. Route 40 into downtown Frederick. She'll find a parking space for the car on East Market, and head into Hendrickson's Bakery, where the chocolate cake (with chocolate frosting) she ordered last week will be ready for pick-up. She'll exchange a few pleasant words with Marie at the bakery, pay, and then return home to the Braddock Heights mansion she and her family have lived in for the past decade. In the large, empty kitchen, she'll unpack the cake, place it on the marble countertop, and decorate it with seven blue candles.

"That's one for every ten years," Patterson says. Appropriately enough, because tomorrow is the seventieth birthday of her husband, Charles Patterson. Though his name does not command the instant recognition it once did outside the Frederick County area, longtime residents will recall Patterson's fifteen minutes of fame in the mid-1970s, when his paintings routinely fetched six-figure sums at auction.

Those same residents may also remember the tragic accident Patterson suffered on July 15, 1984, while on a camping trip with his son, Jeff. An accidental fall resulted in severe head injuries, putting the elder Patterson into a coma from which he has never emerged. In early 1985, Kathleen Patterson brought her husband home from the hospital, setting up a specially equipped room in the basement so that Charles could receive the care he needed in familiar surroundings.

"I didn't want him in a white room somewhere, with strangers coming in once a day to turn him over in bed." Though Patterson has round-the-clock help for her husband, she often sees to his needs herself. She even reads the newspaper to him, and keeps the nearby television tuned to his favorite programs, whenever possible.

Son Jeff, now thirteen years old, helps her out whenever possible: he's usually the one who blows out the candles on his father's cake every year.

"He did so much for me, when I was growing up," Jeff says. "This is the least I can do for him."

Medical experts put Patterson's chances of recovery at practically nil, but the Donovans discount all such negative talk.

"I've read any number of stories where people just suddenly woke up and were fine," says Kathleen Patterson. "I don't see why that can't happen with Charles."

"My mom and I, we'll never give up hope," young Jeff adds. "You just have to believe. All we need is a little bit of magic to go our way."

Frederick Post   established 1846
Volume 143, Number 245

Frederick, Maryland
Thursday, September 1, 1988

# KSP

September 2, 2000

Dear Mr. Stern:

With this letter, I grant you permission to reprint the material you looked at while you were at our house, as well as the material from Jeff's Shelter Glen file. You shouldn't feel bad about Jeff not wanting to talk to you for the book: he won't talk to me either.

Sincerely,

Kathleen Sharrar Patterson

P.S. - Thank you for picking up the cake. That was sweet.

## POSTSCRIPT

You won't find Charles Patterson's paintings in museums.

If you talk to gallery owners in New York City, where Patterson showed most of his work, you'll find that most of his pieces—particularly the later ones—found their way into the hands of private collectors, and are rarely exhibited to the public.

You can find examples of Patterson's early work, if you're willing to expend the effort and pay for the privilege: copies of the pulp magazines featuring his drawings do come up for sale, from time to time.

The original artwork for many of those magazines remains in the possession of his wife, Kathleen Sharrar Patterson. In fact, I saw the cover painting for "The Book of Shadows" very recently, when I went to the Patterson mansion in Braddock Heights at Mrs. Patterson's invitation to discuss her son, Jeff.

That painting is in the basement, hanging over Charles Patterson's bed.

A nurse comes every day to check the readouts of the various machines hooked up to the artist's wasted body, to evaluate his condition, and to turn and stretch his atrophied limbs.

"We'll never give up hope," Jeff Patterson told a newspaper reporter when he was 13.

Picture that young man now, coming down to the basement to sit with his father, perhaps to hold his hand, or to talk to him. At some point, Jeff's gaze inevitably wanders, coming to rest on the painting on the wall.

His father, the painting.

The minutes stretch into hours: the light outside fades, the room grows dark.

His father lying on the bed. His father lying on the rock.

A nine-year-old boy, alone in the woods.

He hears a noise in the darkness.

*Clip-clop, clip-clop.*

When he was a boy, something terrible happened to Jeff Patterson. It made him go a little bit crazy: fact and fiction collided in his head.

He thought he could do magic.

He thought the bogeyman was real.

People see strange things all the time, of course, especially in the woods near Burkittsville, Maryland. That's what Stephen Ryan Parker and Tristen Ryler were writing about: the hype, and the horror. The facts, and the fantasies that grew up around them.

This book is about those fantasies, and the ones Jeff Patterson grew up with.

Hysteria? History? Or something else altogether?

We leave it to you to decide.

Thanks go to:

Ben Rock, for numerous late-night counseling sessions.

Tom Kovar, for expert guidance in matters relating to the workings of the human mind.

Glenn & Gabrielle at Night Owl Books, who supplied the missing pieces for *The Book of Shadows*.

Sheldon Cashdan, whose own book, *The Witch Must Die*, provided invaluable background information relating to "Bloody Sam of Malkin Tower."

Michael Tousman, who sings but does not plaster.

Madeleine Harley Stern, who draws but does not type.

Everyone at Pocket Books: Judith Curr, Kara Welsh, Scott Shannon, Liate Stehlik, and in particular, Linda Dingler, Twisne Fan, Lisa Feuer, Penelope Haynes, and—of course—the Pocket Rocket, for once again making the impossible happen.

At Red Herring: Deb Schuller and Andrea Sepic

At Artisan Entertainment: Amorette Jones, Ferrell McDonald, and Sonia Imparato.

For a great story: Dick Beebe, Joe Berlinger, and Jon Bokenkamp

The brave men who live in the heart of love: Rob Cowie, Mike Monello, Dan Myrick, Eduardo Sanchez, and Gregg Hale.

Extra special thanks to Margaret Clark, who went so far above and beyond on this project that if you search the night sky...

Also:

Erica Blair
Sam Caine
Jennifer Gates
Kara Grenier
Elizabeth P. Hartman
John Mutter
Rachel Plzak
Daniel A. Slater
Cleo Stern (who graciously allowed reproduction of her likeness)

And Jill, who not only saved my bacon, but fried it up just right.

(Moltarr, I'll get you next time.)

More about the author:
http://more.at/dastern